The Letter

by

David E Balaam

Other titles by the same author;

Columbus Day

Nothing is Sacrosanct

No One is Sacrosanct

To Lindsay, my second daughter,

my second novel

PART ONE

There is a crack in everything
That's how the light gets in
L.Cohen

Chapter One

Although Majadahonda is only ten miles from Madrid as the crow flies, it had taken me over three hours to find the damn town. Madrid airport is situated north-east of the city - Majadahonda is north-west of the city. A simple drive around the ring road would surely be easy.

No.

I made the mistake of asking the car hire assistant the best way out of the airport.

"Si. Take the M13, west, then M11 then M607 and follow the signs, easy."

Easy! Like hell.

Driving, and trying to read a map at the same time is not easy. I ended up almost going through the center of Madrid, which I would not recommend to anyone. I found myself instead on the wrong motorway heading south. I did not have an appointment as such, so time was not an issue. I was just frustrated at having to waste petrol, even though I wasn't paying for it. I eventually found the connecting M30 and was reassured to see signs to Majadahonda.

This old town, once just a small farming village, has grown like a Phoenix out of the wilderness in the past twenty years. It is now a desirable up-market suburb of Madrid, which the rich and famous have made their own.

Celebrities, businessmen, diplomats, sports personalities and the nouveau riche, can be found here. Most of the architecture is modern - very modern.

Spain has a wonderful mix of new and old, which sits well together, and Majadahonda is no exception. Mostly laid flat during the civil war, it was neglected for many years until the early 1970's when, with the aid of EEC funding, began to find a new life. The rich and famous wanted to move out of the noisy and overcrowded streets of Madrid, and they slowly started to buy up the cheap land, where they built villas and luxury apartments.

I hoped this would be my final destination. I had visited several countries in six months looking for this lady, and all the signs were that I had finally found the mystery woman my (temporary) employer was so eager for me to make contact with.

I parked in the plaza major and asked for directions to Calle de Fontis. All around me were expensive shops and restaurants, and the café society sat at shaded tables reading, talking, drinking and people watching. I was envious. I wanted to sit there sipping coffee and reflecting on my life, but I had a task to complete, then I could relax once more, back home with my lovely Jayne.

Calle de Fontis is a long, wide, tree-lined cul-de-sac. The stunning villas are nearly all new, although pseudo in style, they are nevertheless impressive.

Number fourteen was towards the end of the street on the north side of the road. I could see beyond the end of the road open land, with a small copse. Very tranquil I thought, but quickly refocused on what I was going to say, if, and when the door opened.

I slowly climbed the polished black stone steps to the equally gleaming polished white double front door and rang the bell. The door was partly glazed with frosted glass but I could see a shadowy figure approach.

The door opened slowly. A young girl in her early teens looked at me curiously, and stood with the door only slightly ajar, ready to close it again quickly.

"Si, Senor," she whispered and squinted in response to the sunlight.

I heard a voice in the background calling to her in Spanish, "Lucie, who is there darling?"

The voice came from an older woman, which was clear and distinctive, but I was hard put to tell the nationality, although the accent seemed Spanish.

"I do not know Grandmamma," the girl replied in Spanish, still in a whispered voice.

My Spanish was not conversational, just enough to order beer and tapas, so I went with English and smiled. "Hola. I am looking for Dianne Greenway, por favor."

I stared at the girl, who did not move or respond, hoping for a reaction. This was going to be harder than I thought.

I was about to repeat the question, this time in some broken Spanish when I heard the other woman's voice coming from behind the girl, but closer to her this time, although I could still not see her.

"Who is asking for Dianne Greenway?" The question was in English and took me by surprise, and I hesitated a few seconds before regaining my concentration.

"Madam, err, Senora, I have been looking for Dianne Greenway on the instructions of my client in England."

There was a silence for what seemed like forever. The next question came more measured and inquisitively.

"Who is your client, and why would this person know Dianne Greenway?"

I thought quickly. I needed to see this woman. I had a feeling, after all this time, I was finally at journey's end. My heart was pounding fast.

"Senora, my client is dying, and as for why I am here, I can only reveal that to the lady in question."

I ground my teeth, hoping I had said enough to gain entrance. A hand appeared on the young girl's shoulder, and a woman slowly emerged out of the shadows of the shaded hallway.

. . .

Michael Parker was in agony. He had not taken his last batch of tablets and was now regretting it.

"I think I'll go to bed with a bottle of whisky and take all the tablets there," he said out loud. He was alone in the house so it did not matter what he said. He did, however, mean it.

The last few months had been getting worse. Treatment had stopped six weeks ago.

"Sorry, Mr Parker," the consultant had said, "the treatment is not working. I am afraid we can do no more except make you as comfortable as possible," and then continued to relate all the options open to a patient who was going to die of cancer.

He was actually sincere in his deliverance, but Michael had stopped listening after the first three words. "Sorry, Mr Parker". Michael knew the rest. He knew in his heart weeks ago he was fighting a losing battle. He could only think of one thing now. James must find her, and find her soon. Time was running out.

Chapter Two

Michael Parker was a successful business-man, husband and father, but for all his success and modest wealth, he now felt alone and empty.

His wife, Rachel, had died tragically five years ago from a bee sting. On average ten people each year die from an allergic reaction to a bee sting. Relatives and friends at the funeral would say, "It was a one in a million chance, Michael, it's not your fault." Michael knew that. Of course, it wasn't his fault. Just a tragic accident, like so many tragic accidents that happen all over the world every day. Although, he thought, it was not strictly an "accident". An accident is something that happens when you know it is happening; like being run over, or having a ladder fall on you. Rachel did not know she had been stung. He told himself in future he would not use the word accident - misfortune was more appropriate he thought.

Michael's son, Charlie was devastated, as were his wife Helen and their children, Michael Jnr. and Elizabeth. After the funeral, back at Charlie and Helen's house, Michael wandered off into his son's study. Like his own it was a quiet place for reading, listening to music and reflection. He sat at the desk in the comfortable leather chair and closed his eyes. He could hear the din of the gathering from beyond the study where he had heard the same commiserations so many times that morning.

He wanted to be alone for a while, and he knew no one would object today.

The problem with being alone at a time like this is that you can't help recalling the past – reminiscing, searching the mind for all the good things that you shared over the years; holidays, parties, marriages, births and just being together.

Michael knew he had had a good marriage, and said a silent "thank you" to Rachel for the good times they had been together.

From the reflection on the computer screen, he could see his great-granddaughter, Zoe, who was just four years old, open the study door and tiptoe towards him.

As she got closer, Michael swung the chair around and surprised her. "Saw you," he said smiling and swept her up on to his lap.

Zoe looked puzzled. "How did you see me, Granddad?"

"Did you not know I have eyes in the back of my head?"

"Daddy has as well!" she exclaimed. "Will I have them when I grow up?" she asked in all seriousness.

"You know what my love, I really believe you might," and she slid off his lap onto the floor. As she walked to the door she turned and said in a gentle innocent voice. "Is Grandma with the angels Granddad?"

Michael smiled and swallowed, and just about stopped a tear forming in his left eye. "I think she is Zoe, I really do."

"I do as well, Granddad. Are you coming back to the party?"

Michael frowned and smiled at this wonderful innocent child standing before him. Where people gather to eat and drink, it must be a party. The innocent logic of a child was faultless.

"I will be in soon," he replied, smiling reassuringly. Zoe left and closed the door, and Michael returned to his memories. Far in the back of his mind, he had compartments for memories.

We all have, but some of us are better than others with storage and retrieval. Michael started to keep thoughts, or memories, stored like this after seeing a memory act many years ago. He was fascinated by the ability the man had for remembering anything; dates, names, places - anything that was thrown at him, he knew the answer. Michael met up with the same entertainer a few years later and spoke at length to him about his unique talent.

The man had smiled, and after hesitating momentarily, informed Michael it was not a God-given talent, but he had learnt the art of remembering.   He was so enamored with Michael's interest he told him his "secret" there and then.

Discipline is the key. The mind has to be disciplined to accept information stored in a particular way, and in a way that it can be retrieved. The least important memories are kept in the back of the mind, like keeping old books on the very top shelf or abandoned clothes in one corner of the wardrobe.

You might say that is what we do with any information we don't use a lot - true, but if it is stored randomly it will take longer to retrieve, especially in later life; then you will be labelled with memory loss when you could so easily have retrieved what you wanted.

Michael had "pigeon-holed" many such old memories and was starting to filter them out when one, either consciously or otherwise, came slowly forward from the darkness of his storage vaults, from the very back of his mind, and sat there, waiting to be opened, like Pandora's Box.

Michael shuddered and opened his eyes as if waking from a disturbed sleep. Had he been dreaming? No, the memory was still there.

He knew of course what was in it, but he had not summoned this one intentionally. He felt ashamed. It was not what he wanted to remember, on today of all days.

He tried to clear his mind and return the memory to the designated corner of his mind, but the more he tried the more it kept coming forward and forward until he had to open it. And there she was - Dianne. It may have been over forty years, but once the box was opened, the memory was as fresh as if they had met yesterday. The study door opened again and this time Helen put her head around the door, and whispered, almost mouthing the sentence. "Are you OK, shall I send Charlie in?"

Michael smiled back but could not rid himself of the memory that now occupied his mind.

"I'm fine thank you, Helen, I will re-join the . . ." he was about to say party but stopped himself. Helen would not understand, "I will re-join you all in a minute."

Satisfied he was alright, Helen closed the door as quietly as she could, "OK, Michael, we understand."

Michael stood up and pushed Dianne as far as he could to the back of his mind. "Today is not about you, Dianne. Go away."

Now, five years later, he had been given the news he had skin cancer. He had had biopsies on three moles, all of which turned out to be malignant. He was put on a course of chemotherapy which would last for three months, and if he did not have the "all clear", or something close to it, the prognosis would not be good.

News of this magnitude focuses the mind, but Michael was not one to panic or fret. He let others do that. He would not "give in" as others put it, but if his time was up then he was at peace with that.

Certainly better, he thought, than a sudden death with no warning. No time to *put things in order*" or "*right any wrongs*".

He was not sure why he had thought that: right any wrongs, but the more he said the phrase over in his mind, the clearer it became. Dianne. Michael, in fact, did not have unpleasant memories of Dianne. On the contrary, their brief relationship of just six months was a joyous occasion. It was 1965. They had met while Michael was visiting the British Museum in London one wet and cold Monday during his lunch hour. He was in a section of the Egyptian room eating a sandwich, sitting on one of four semi-circular stone benches, staring at a giant obelisk.

"Do you like that?" he heard from behind him. He turned to see a pretty young woman looking at him, her head cocked, expecting an answer. He was tongue-tied and did not like being at a disadvantage. "Err... I am not sure. It's very large," was all he could manage. She stepped over the bench and sat next to him. Her smile was infectious.

"Not the bloody Hatshepsut obelisk, the sandwich. Do you want it? I'm starving," he gave it to her willingly, and she devoured it.

"Don't they feed you here?" He saw a museum badge pinned to her cardigan so assumed she was staff.

"Yes," she said, wiping her mouth on the paper napkin from his lunch box, "but they don't pay holiday students, and its miles back to the canteen, even I get lost."

Michael smiled, and they both laughed.

For the rest of that week Michael shared his lunch with Dianne in the Egyptian room. They talked about what she was doing there, and what he did, and by Friday he had asked her out. "Can I buy you a proper meal tomorrow?"

She smiled her smile and kissed him on the mouth. "You can take that as a yes."

Their relationship was passionate. They made love on every occasion, and each time was better than before. They would lie on her single bed after making love and share a cigarette, and listen to Bob Dylan, Neil Young or Leonard Cohen. She was twenty-four and he was twenty-eight, and they didn't have a care in the world. By the end of the summer she was to return to university in Leicester to complete her studies in Archaeology. Michael had thought it through, and he would visit her every weekend.

On the week of her leaving he called round to her rooms in Bayswater, where she shared a house with two others. One was a student studying law who had rooms on the top floor, one above Dianne, and the other was a backpacking Aussie touring Europe but had not moved on since moving in three months ago. Her name was Pamela, and Michael did not get on with her at all.

"Hi, Mike," she said, in her usual greeting, hovering outside her room on the ground floor. Michael had stopped trying to correct her in the use of this hated abbreviation of his name, but she now did it on purpose just to annoy him.

"Di's not here if you are looking for her," she said, in her coarse Melbourne accent.

Michael dismissed the information and walked passed her, and jogged up the stairs two at the time. He knocked on Dianne's door and turned the handle but it was locked.

Pamela had followed him upstairs. "Told you she wasn't here." She said smugly.

"Pamela, don't play games, where is she?" Michael was staring daggers at her, letting her know he was serious.

"Don't talk to me like that, Mike, you're not wanted here anymore."

Michael stood back in shock. "What did you say? What are you talking about?"

"She's gone, and she won't be back afterwar ." Pamela stopped herself.

"Afterwards . . . is that what you were going to say? Tell me woman . . . after what!" Michael was shouting now. "After what!"

Pamela turned to go downstairs, but Michael caught her hand on the top step and held her, as if to let her fall if he wanted to. Pamela shouted back. "Leave me alone – haven't you done enough damage?"

Michael steadied the woman and released his grip. "What damage, tell me for God's sake, Pamela." His voice was quieter now, but his expression was one of grave concern.

Pamela said nothing for while – dragging out the suspense, preferring to stare at the ground. "She was pregnant. She's having it out." She looked at him impassively but was bracing herself for the response.

It came. "You're lying, you jealous dyke, you're lying. Where is she?" he grabbed her again and started to shake her. He felt a hand on his shoulder which pulled him around.

"Hey, leave her alone Michael. What's going on here?" It was the student from the top floor flat.

"This bitch . . ." Michael started to say.

"Stop calling me that," Pamela shouted back, staring at him squarely.

Michael turned back to the student. "She says Di was pregnant. What do you know? Tell me she's lying." He demanded, panic now resonating in his voice.

"Sorry, I can't help you, Michael. I think you had better leave now." The young man said coolly, without expression, but looking beyond Michael towards Pamela.

"Surely you must have heard something. How come she knows and not you?"

The student just shrugged. "Come on, let's all go downstairs," he said, and he and Pamela started down the stairs, leaving Michael at the top, still trying to understand what was going on.

Realizing they had moved, Michael followed them down. The two stood in the narrow hallway whispering. As Michael approached, Pamela just gave a sarcastic smile.

"Please," he begged to both of them, "when she returns get her to call me. I will be at home," he left the house, still in a daze, and walked towards his Lambretta.

He sat for over an hour watching the front door of the flat in case Dianne came back. He could see her bedroom window on the first floor, but there was no sign of movement. Eventually, he drove off, his mind still full of questions, realizing he may never see her again. Every hour he telephoned her. He did this for the next five days until the others got fed up and left the phone off the hook.

Days turned to weeks, and weeks into months and still with no word from her.

Michael eventually got back to normality, but he never accepted Dianne was pregnant. Why had she left so suddenly? And why not tell him, whatever the reason? Why didn't she leave a note?

Their relationship had been so intense they had not talked about each other's families, or the past. They lived for the moment, enjoying life, and the summer of "65".

All that was a long time ago and Dianne had been placed in storage in the back of Michael's mind for over forty years. Until, that is, she had crept her way forward and forward until he could no longer ignore her.

Chapter Three

Michael was now consumed with memories of Dianne, and, maybe having not long to live, decided to do something about it.

He had made his Will many years ago, and as he prospered he had added beneficiaries here and there when he thought someone was deserving of his goodwill. The last time he had met with Morris, Sterne and Wicks, the family solicitors, was after the death of his wife. Rachel had been a director of the company and they had separate Wills. They had agreed, however, they would leave the bulk of the estate to each other, and if they died together, everything was to go to their son, with the usual exceptions such as relatives and friends. Rachel, however, had included in her Will beneficiaries such as the local gardening club, the art club, the local school and her housekeeper, Smithy, who had worked for them for over thirty years.

He was determined then and there to spend some of his hard-earned cash on one final quest. And maybe die, finally knowing the truth about Dianne's disappearance all those years ago.

. . .

The offices of Morris, Sterne and Wicks, in Notting Hill, had grown over the years. A reflection on their success, due in part to their specialist area in company Law and Litigation, which was most lucrative. They also had a very good Will and Probate office, which had been headed by the late Mr Sterne.

"Mr Lacey." The call was more a command than a request. "Here, now please." The command had come from the now most senior partner Mr Morris, head of the practice, and an excellent solicitor in Law.

I had been junior clerk to the late Mr Sterne, in Wills and Probate. I am James Lacey.

"Yes, sir," I said as I entered Morris's office. Morris was reading through a file. "Sit," he said, without looking up from his notes.

I had become used to Morris's "command speech". He spoke like that to everyone. Some of the staff would joke behind his back that he spoke to his wife like that. "Can you imagine," they would say, "old Morris giving his wife commands. "Bed", "Undress", "Hold" . . ." and they all laughed.

Mr Sterne, on the other hand, despite his name, had been the opposite. Kind, gentle and very approachable. Everyone was saddened by his death, but I was especially sad, not just because I worked with him, but I really liked the man and had looked upon him as a mentor.

"Your workload will increase somewhat. Can you cope?" Morris had not looked up from the file he was reading.

"It will be difficult sir. Are we . . . you . . . looking to replace Mr Sterne, and find a new partner in Probate?"

Morris finally looked up from the file and removed his spectacles. "How long have you been with us, Mr Lacey?"

"Almost eighteen months, sir."

"Do you like it here"?

"Yes, sir, very much. I was hoping to . . ." but was stopped mid-sentence.

"Good. Mr Wicks will cover Probate for a while, and we will take on a temporary clerk. I have something I want you to do."

I was intrigued. I thought Morris was going to just pile more work on me until they replaced poor Mr Sterne.

"Do you know our client Mr Michael Parker, of Parker & Son?"

I thought a moment trying to recall some of the clients. "I think I have seen the name on the system, but I have had no dealings with them."

"This is the Will file for Mr Parker," handing me the buff file he was reading. "Mr Parker has requested a visit to make changes to his Will. I want you to visit him at his home in Guildford. Can you handle that?"

I was starting to read the file. "Yes, sir. When does he want to see me?"

"As soon as possible he told me, which means something else has happened in the family since the death of his wife." Morris was thoughtful. "He has been a good client over the years, so get down there as soon as you can. That's all."

I rose obediently to the command. Morris called out as I reached the door.

"Mr Lacey, don't forget to keep all receipts otherwise you cannot reclaim expenses."

Back in my office, I read through the file more closely. Michael Parker had been with the firm for over forty-five years and had not only his company business with them but also his personal undertakings. I read through a copy of the Last Will and Testament of Mr Michael Parker.

Nothing unusual here. Probably decided to leave something to the local cat's home. I can see this being a waste of time and thought it could have been done over the phone. I looked at my "IN" tray, then back at the Parker file. "Guildford it is then."

I telephoned Michael Parker and arranged to meet him in two days'. He had sounded very "matter of fact", and had not given any hint of the reason for the meeting.

When I casually suggested if what he wanted could be conducted over the phone, he just insisted he preferred a visit, and why could not Mr Morris come himself. I assured him I would be there as arranged.

. . .

I live with my girlfriend, Jayne, who is twenty-four and is a marketing assistant for one of the brand managers at Glaxo, on the Slough Business Park. We had met at a party two years ago and just "clicked", as Jayne would say. I'd like to think it was also something to do with the fact she reminded me of a petite pixie. Just five foot four, short auburn hair and the widest brown eyes you have ever seen – we had talked all night and when we kissed goodbye, I knew she was special.

Within six months we had found a flat and moved in. Jayne's parents were not happy at first. Before they had met me they had built a picture of what I would be like - a typical white middle-class attitude, in response I suspect, on hearing a description of me from Jayne.

I had grown up with these attitudes, and even in today's multi-racial society I still come across people with preconceived conceptions of what they expect me to look, and be like. Most are always surprised on meeting me. I am indeed from an immigrant bloodline.

My grandparents came to the UK in 1946 just before the partition of India fearing the worst was to come, and wanting a better life for their yet unborn child, my mother. My grandparents loved England, and what was considered unusual in those days, embraced English society and culture, but without forfeiting their religious beliefs.

Consequently, my mother was brought up in English ways and customs, while being taught her parents' faith, but did not have any of the strict rules and regulations of her religion enforced on her. She was able to choose her destiny, and it was to meet and marry my father, who was a young white man just out of University, training to be a dentist.

It was a low-key wedding with not many guests. Even close friends of her parents were afraid to attend in case they were seen as approving of a mixed-marriage. Nevertheless, my mum and dad were very happy and lived a quiet, comfortable life. She worked in a solicitor's office, and dad built up a good dental practice. I was born three years later. When I was nine years old my father died suddenly of a tumor on the brain. Everyone was devastated. Mother mourned for months, as was the custom, but she was also doing it out of love for her husband, not just duty. Mother inherited what was then a small fortune. Certainly enough to keep her, me and her parents in comfort forever. Following in my mother's liberal upbringing I was also allowed the freedom later in life to choose my path in society, and instinctively chose that of the country I had been born and raised in. I was English by birth and therefore I am an Englishman.

By the time I reached eighteen, however, mother had decided to suddenly revert to her maiden name of Sharjeel, without any explanation.

The reality was, however, she wanted to find another husband, and this time she was looking amongst the Asian community. Eventually she did remarry, but I did not get on with my step-father and vowed never to take his name.

I was also convinced he was after mother's money. I left soon afterwards for University but had deep concerns about leaving her alone with her new husband.

Chapter Four

I arrived exactly on time. I had always been a good time-keeper. Mother always said that if one had an appointment with God you would not want to be late, so why be late for anyone else. I am not sure I understood the complete logic of her astuteness, but it has held me in good stead for being punctual.

The door was opened by an elderly woman, with a stern expression. "Yes."

"My name is James Lacey. I have an appointment with Mr Michael Parker."

She opened the door wider so I could enter, but said nothing more, although I could tell she was studying me – summing me up.

The entrance hall was large and square with a flight of stairs straight ahead, and with two doors leading off to the right, and one at the end of the corridor.

"Wait here." She said and went through the second door on the right.

I stood and waited. Just inside the hall was a large coat stand holding several coats, suitable for all weather conditions. Next to that was a large white ceramic umbrella holder with one umbrella and three walking sticks. An oval mirror with a dark mahogany frame hung on the wall opposite the coat stand. I checked my tie and hair. Both were perfect.

"Mr Parker will see you now." I jumped. The elderly woman was suddenly standing next to me, and I am sure I saw the faintest of smiles on her wrinkled lips. I followed her into the furthest room. "Don't tire him out," she whispered, now expressionless, and closed the door behind her.

"Don't take any notice of her," I heard a voice somewhere in the dim room, "my hearing is still perfect. It's the rest of me that's falling apart. Come here man, I can't see you. Come and sit down opposite."

I negotiated a nest of coffee tables and saw Michael Parker sitting in a high backed comfortable chair. He was dressed in pajamas and a dressing-gown, and I realized then he was not a well man. All around him were dozens of pill containers and bottles of what I assumed was medicine.

"Come here – I don't bite, and take no notice of all this paraphernalia. It's all worthless." Michael insisted. I stood in front of the man and felt I was being judged, yet again.

"You're young. How old are you?" Michael asked in a matter of fact way.

"Twenty-eight in December, sir." I knew that would surprise him. It always did when I told someone my age. It is said I look five years younger, which was good in some ways, but a curse in others.

Michael, however, did not flinch at the answer.

"How long have you been with Morris's lot?"

"Eighteen months, sir. I worked with Mr Sterne before he died," I replied, and added for no particular reason, "poor man."

Michael was expressionless. "Yes, he was OK I suppose . . ." he said, looking away a moment as if thinking. "More manners than that Morris fellow. Never did like him," he finally said. "Sit down man, sit down," he demanded as if talking to a pet.

I looked behind me and sat in an identical high backed chair facing Michael Parker, and started to take a file out of my briefcase.

"You won't need that. Just a pen and pad to take notes, unless you have one of those Dictaphone things."

"No sir, pen and pad it is, but don't you want to talk about your will?" I asked with interest.

Michal was silent for a while, and I just sat and waited. He looked older than seventy-five, with a gaunt expression, probably due to whatever was ailing him. He had deep-set blue eyes and thinning mousy-colored hair. He removed his thick-rimmed glasses and stared beyond me. I could see he was struggling to relate what he wanted to tell me, and after a moment I took my eyes off the muted man and surveyed the room.

We were in semi-darkness for some reason, and from what I could see as my eyes became accustomed to the dimness, was that the room was very tastefully decorated - full of furniture and bookshelves.

Michael Parker was very much aware of what he wanted to say but sat studying the young man in front of him. Was I old enough, or experienced enough to undertake a wild goose chase? How would I feel about leaving home for an undetermined length of time? Am I married? Am I gay? Who would miss me? Probably his mother, Michael thought, looking at me again.

Looks a mother's boy.

"Do you have a passport?" Michael eventually asked.

I turned, startled by the question. "Yes. . . I have a passport. Is that relevant?"

"It could well be, young man. It could well be," he confirmed, almost smiling, pushing back some whispers of hair behind his ear.

"Let me tell you why I asked Morris to send you over." He said thoughtfully. "My wife died as you know. We had been married for forty years and we have a son, Charlie. I built up my father's business making furniture, and in the past fifteen years Charlie extended the business to mass-produce hotel furniture, which has been very successful, and made us all very rich." He paused to reflect. "You can take notes if you want to," he added pointing to the pad.

"I'm OK for now, sir, most of that is in the file I have read about your company."

"Good. I'm glad you have done some homework. But now this is a story that is not documented," he paused again and took a deep breath.

"Many years ago, in 1965, when I was a young man, around your age, I met a young woman. Her name was Dianne Holland. She was studying archaeology at Leicester University, and we met at the British Museum where she was on holiday work experience. We clicked immediately - love at first sight I suppose you could say. It was a passionate affair, and neither of us knew if it would last or not. We spent our free days out of London on my Lambretta, usually in Brighton or somewhere on the coast. Mostly I stayed at her flat. I was living at home so it was more convenient." He paused again for a sip of water. Smiling at a memory.

"We made love at every opportunity, and we would lie in bed listening to Neil Young or James Taylor all night, or until we fell asleep in each other's arms."

Here was a man I have never met relating a most private moment in his life. A wonderful memory. A time of close intermittency. Could I do that? Talk about Jayne and me like that to a stranger.

"Are you OK?" I heard Michael ask.

"Yes, sorry. Thinking how lovely that sounded."

"Ah, I see you are a romantic as well. Romance is the secret to a good partnership – and good sex," he added, and laughed to ease my embarrassment, I think.

"We both loved the songs of Dylan and others like him, and one particular singer I introduced her to was Leonard Cohen. Do you know of him?"

I shook my head. "Not really. But I have seen the name somewhere".

"Yes, he did a World Tour in 2008 at the age of seventy-four. He had a band with him and singers, but back in the early days he just sang and played the guitar. He was a poet, and his voice was . . . how can I say . . . an acquired taste. Rough some would say, but to his fans it was the words, not the singing that was important, and that made him special. He was a very prolific writer, and said what had to be said, whether they were anti-war protest songs or love songs." He smiled at more memories, and I wrote the name on my pad. I now had two entries. Dianne Holland. Leonard Cohen.

"I brought her several LP's of Cohen. Now, of course, it's all CD's, but I have kept all my originals," he said, pointing to a shelf behind me. "Go, go have a look if you want."

I welcomed the chance to stretch my legs, so I looked over the hundreds of vinyl LP's neatly laid out on three shelves. There must have been two hundred of them. People I had almost never heard of, except the occasional Bob Dylan, The Beatles and of course now Leonard Cohen. Others included Pete Seeger, Peter, Paul and Mary, Joan Biaz and one other I did recognize, Ravi Shankar. "I do know this man. My mother liked his music." I said too excitedly, holding the cover aloft.

"Ah, yes Ravi. He brought Asian music to the West. A great musician. Can you see the Leonard Cohen album called The Future?"

I flipped through a dozen or so before I saw the white album cover with an unusual design; a white dove above a heart, over a pair of handcuffs.

I passed the record sleeve to Michael. "Some of my favorite lyrics are on this record." He took the inner sleeve from inside the cover that listed the words to all twelve songs. "Ah, here it is. The Anthem." He scanned the lyrics mouthing the words, while I just sat there, feeling this was becoming rather surreal.

"This was not out when Dianne and I were together, but I love the words in this song,

Ring the bells that still can ring
Forget your perfect offering
There is a crack in everything
That's how the light gets in

"There is a crack in everything, that's how the light gets in," he repeated the last two lines. "Don't you think that's true? He is saying everything, including us, has a crack, a chink in our armor if you like, that allows others to see our inner self. Nothing can be hidden from the light." Michael leant back and breathed heavily, giving me concern for this health.

"Are you OK, sir, shall I get someone?"

"No, I'm fine. It's just that memories can be more emotional than you expect sometimes, I'm fine. I must finish telling you what happened."

I don't know if his explanation of the lyrics was correct, but he seemed to believe it, and I do know that a man's beliefs are everything, especially as we get older. I was not there to judge Michael Parker, just to listen, and the more I did, the more I became drawn into this man's furtive past.

"We are nearly done. Let me continue. One day it suddenly all ended. I learnt, from her flatmate, she had suddenly up and left – no explanation – no note or letter, nothing. I did not believe the woman at first, but as time went on Dianne never re-appeared."

"What did you do to find her?" I asked without thinking.

Michael looked at me harshly, then smiled and shrugged. "On reflection, not enough. We hardly knew anything about each other - as I said, it was a passionate affair."

I nodded as if I knew what he meant.

"The reason I was given by her flatmate was that she was pregnant."

I fidgeted in the chair, and for some reason felt uncomfortable. I looked down at my notepad and added 'pregnant'.

I now had a list: Dianne Holland. Leonard Cohen. Pregnant. Little did I know how intertwined they would all become. Michael did not comment on my discomfort, and when I had finished writing he continued.

"I did contact the university, but they would not give out any information on students. But it will be a good starting point for you."

I looked at him inquisitively. "Starting point! You want me to go to Leicester?"

"Mr Lacey, or can I call you James. Yes, I want you to try and find Dianne Holland, wherever she is, and I mean wherever. "

It took me a while to comprehend what he was asking me to do. "Mr Parker, you want me to find this lady, and you do not know if she is even alive, or if she is, where in the world she is living."

"That about sums it up, James," he said, and frowned, waiting for my response.

I leant back in the chair and closed my eyes. "This is a job for a detective," I stated, leaning forward again, staring him face on.

 "I am a solicitor's clerk. How can I achieve this?"

Michael looked drained. I don't think he had thought about the logistics of such an undertaking by someone like me. I could, I suppose, make some initial enquiry for Death Certificates, or at the University, which was a long shot, but if that will keep him happy for a couple of days then I can get back to my real work. What was old man Morris thinking? Did he even agree to this?

My thoughts were interrupted. "James, I know this may seem like a wild goose chase, but please indulge me. I am dying. I have skin cancer, and have only about six months to live."

That was news to me. Morris did not say anything about him dying but would explain all the medicine in the room.

"I am sorry to hear that . . . I . . . am really sorry," was all I could offer.

He raised his hand. "Do not be concerned. I have accepted my fate. We all die one day - it's just a matter of how we die that is important. I want to die at home with familiar things around me, not in a sterile hospice, no matter how good they are."

 This news did put a different complexion on things. A man's dying wish and all that . . . I took a deep breath. "Did the flatmate confirm Dianne was pregnant?"

His face brightened to my apparent interest. "No. Not at all, that's why I thought she was lying. She claimed there was no letter either," he said, suddenly looking serious again.

"Strange about that woman. I didn't like her from the beginning, but ending up as she did . . . well, it's not something you would wish on anyone."

I was feeling lost now. "What happened, sir, to the Australian woman?"

"She died of an overdose a month after Dianne left. I remember she tried to get Dianne to smoke pot back then, but she never did."

"What did the police do or say. Did they suspect anything other than an overdose?"

Parker shot me a look. "Why do you ask that, or is it your legal side talking?"

I sat back in my chair not sure where to go with this, but Parker continued, unprompted. "They did question everyone, including me. The . . . young student on the top floor must have given them my details. They also tried to trace Dianne for questioning but gave up after a week. The inquest returned a verdict of accidental death as they had found some sleeping pills and a quantity of marijuana she had been smoking."

"Are you saying she committed suicide, and it wasn't an accident?" I asked in amazement.

Parker shrugged. "We will never know. But it does not detract from the matter at hand - finding Dianne Holland."

A thought crossed my mind. "Mr Parker. You do realize she could be dead as well, or anywhere in the world."

"Yes, of course. And regards abroad, that's why I asked about the passport," he said with a now mischievous smile. Before I could think again he pointed to the table. "Over there. On the table is everything you will need. An envelope contains spending money, and there's more if you need it.

The other is a sealed letter I want you to give her if you find her. That's all I ask of you."

He leant back and closed his eyes, now drained of memories. I went to the table and opened the unsealed envelope marked 'Expenses'.

It contained £500 in five-pound notes. I also picked up the second envelope, an A5 manila, with a beautiful copperplate script with just one word, Dianne. Feeling the content I deduced it contained several pages of memories and questions. Questions that may never be answered.

Looking over my shoulder I saw Michael Parker was asleep. I collected my briefcase and packed the notepad and the two envelopes into it and zipped it shut.

I still had questions to ask - like, what did his son think of this quest to find an old lover, and maybe take a share of the family fortune. I realized then I was already involved, and part of me wanted to know if Dianne Holland was dead or alive.

Chapter Five

I took my notepad out on the train back to London and jotted down some more notes.

Leicester University From? to 1965
Archaeology - Which area?
If had child, where born?

Not much to go on and where to start? Leicester I suppose, then what? I made a call to my friend Jonathan Llewellyn-Jones, or Porky to his friends. He works at Frasier & Frasier who specialize in tracing people who may have been left an inheritance.

"Hi, Jamie, what's up friend? Left that lovely lady yet?" He knows calling me Jamie winds me up, and he has a yearning for Jayne.

"Hi, Johnny boy," he dislikes that as much as I hate Jamie. "I'm fine, and so is Jayne. Listen, I'm on a train so reception may not last long. Can I come and see you tomorrow. I need a favor."

"In that case make in lunchtime. See you around one . . ." and the line went dead.

Next morning, back in my office in Notting Hill, I reported to Mr Morris.

He sat silent for ten minutes listening to my report on Michael Parker's story, and his request to me to find Dianne Holland. When I finished he still said nothing. Just staring at me as if I was mad.

"Good God!" He said eventually. "Old man Parker has a bastard . . . that's going to put the cat amongst the pigeons, and we will have to sort it out . . ." he trailed off, staring into space, considering the consequences of a claim to an inheritance.

"Sir, Mr Morris, we don't know about the child yet. It could have been malicious gossip." I said, trying to bring him back to reality.

"Yes, yes of course," he said, refocusing on me again. "So, he gave you £500 expenses. Where does he expect you to go - Scotland?" And gave a nervous laugh.

"Well, there's more money if I need it. He wants me to leave no stone unturned . . . but that's looking ahead. I am going to visit a friend at Frasier and Frasier to see if he can help trace Dianne Holland, and I will also call Leicester University to see if they can be of help. Apart from that . . ." And shrugged to show I was out of ideas.

Morris looked concerned. "The Parker family are good clients, so we must be seen to help in every way." He stood up and came around the large wooden desk towards me. I instinctively stood and looked down from my 5ft 11in to his 5ft 4in balding crown. (This is the reason, we assume, he never usually stands up in his office.) I suppressed a wicked grin and took a step backwards.

"James . . . spend the rest of the week on this and we will appraise the situation next Monday. That's all for now," and he went back to his chair. I was frozen momentarily. He has never called me James. He never uses first names, to anyone. This must be important to him, and I felt slightly privileged to be entrusted with the task.

At least it got me out of the office. It was early May, a great time of year to be in London. Not too cold, not too hot.

Summer clothes are starting to make an appearance after the warmer wear of the late spring. People also seem happier and content when the sun shines. That said, my old friend, Porky, was happy and content whatever the time of year – as long as he had a pint in his hand. His two passions in life are Rugby and Beer, but I'm not sure in which order. It would also include flirting, but I don't think that's a legitimate pastime.

I arrived at his Covent Garden office at 12.45. "Good timing James . . . just thinking of lunch."

"Nothing new then," I replied, "but I think we should talk first. I want you with a clear head."

He looked hurt. "Jamie . . . sorry James . . . that will cost you the first round and a date with your lovely lady."

"Happy to oblige the first, but you will just have to admire from afar for the second"

"So, tell all . . . what's this about?"

Again, I told the story of Michael Parker to a silent audience. "Bloody hell, man. He got you looking for this woman from nearly fifty years ago who had a love child - juicy one," he said with glee, rubbing his hands. "So where do we start?" he said looking at his laptop. He keyed some commands and the screen displayed a matrix of boxes waiting to be filled.

"OK," he took a deep breath "Name."

"Dianne Holland," I confirmed and opened my notebook to help recall the other information I had gathered.

"Date of Birth +/- 5 years," he asked next.

"In that case go with 1945."

"Fine. Now, place of birth." Silence. "Hey, James. Place of birth."

'That's all I have on her."

He leant back in his chair. "You don't make my job any easier do you," he said with a grin. "I don't think we will find her just on this, but let's see what comes up," he pressed the keypad, and the screen changed to a blank screen for a few seconds. Then a list of names, all Dianne Holland, with their date of birth next to them, appeared. 2,465 in total.

"Wow," I exclaimed, "that's a lot of names."

"Agreed, and we would normally narrow the search further by demographic information, but we don't seem to have any, do we, my friend," he said, giving me a sarcastic look.

We both sat staring at the computer screen as if by some magical intervention it would pop-up the details we wanted.

"OK," Jonathan said, ready to make an important observation. "I suggest we continue this in the pub," and with that he picked up the laptop and I followed him out into the bright sunlight.

When I got back to our table with a pint of Pride and a pint of orange juice, Jonathan was tapping away at the laptop again. "What's that?" he asked, seeing my non-alcoholic drink.

"I'm working, even if you're not. I want to keep a clear head today."

"That hurts. I'm always working." He took a good long swig of the beer and his face lit up. "That's better.

First one of the day is always the best. Now, how do we solve a problem like Dianne," and he stared again at his screen. "Are you sure he didn't mention where she came from. Anything. An accent perhaps."

I thought for a moment, but my blank expression told him his answer.

"I am going to try the Uni again. I know Parker said he called, but that was back then. Perhaps if I go in person they may be more forthcoming."

"Good idea. You don't even have to use a cover story. You are trying to trace someone who, as a solicitor, wants to contact someone with information to their advantage."

He beamed, pleased with his analysis.

. . .

I was disappointed Jonathan's efforts had not turned up anything to go on, but it is early days. What had I missed? I had a name but that was all. I decided to go to Leicester to see if that would throw up any new evidence. The previous evening back at our flat I had told Jayne of my visit to Michael Parker, and the quest he had asked me to perform. Her reaction was much the same as everyone else. "Why on earth does he want to drag up the past now?"

"Because he is dying for one, and he can afford it for another," I replied, sounding slightly too flippant.

She was not very convinced. "And just how long are you going to spend on this quest as you call it. And from what you say you could be away for days on end," she added, looking forlorn at the prospect of being left alone.

"I do not plan to be away long at all. Morris has given me until Friday to see what I can discover, and we will decide how to proceed on Monday. If I can't turn anything up by then I will tell old man Parker it is a fruitless quest." She came over to me and we hugged silently. "You won't be looking for any old girlfriends when we are old and grey will you?" she asked seriously.

"You are my first and last," I said and kissed her reassuringly. She looked at me slyly. "Your first, I doubt it, but I like the sound of being the last," and she hugged me even tighter.

. . .

I thought about phoning the university first, but as Jonathan said, confronting someone in person can often produce better results than a phone conversation.

I caught the 9.30am train to take advantage of the cheap day return, from St. Pancras and arrived in Leicester at 11.00am.

I then took a taxi to the Uni and located the administration offices. Having explained briefly my purpose for being there, and on completing the visitor's record book, I was given a campus pass complete with lanyard and directed to the Student Record Office. From there I was pointed in the direction of Undergraduate Student Records Officer and Bursary Officer. The lady in charge of that section was Ms Samantha Lemon. "Ms Lemon, thank you for seeing me," and I handed her my business card from Morris, Sterne and Wicks.

"So, how can I help you, Mr Lacey? I understand you are looking for a student."

"Yes," I hesitated . . . suddenly not feeling as confident as I thought I would have.

"Yes, we have been instructed to find a lady by the name of Dianne Holland. Unfortunately, we do not know a lot about her, but we do know she was a student here back in around 1965."

Ms Lemon's eyes widened. "1965! Wow . . . I don't know if we have records going back that far, Mr Lacey," and blinked several times through her large round tortoiseshell framed glasses.

"I know it's a long shot, but we have to start somewhere," I continued, not wanting her to dismiss me in the first two minutes. To my relief she leant forward and tapped the computer keyboard. "OK, let me see. What is the name again? Dianne . . ."

"Dianne Holland. Archaeology student." I confirmed.

It was the same procedure Jonathan had undertaken, and all I could do was wait.

Ms Lemon, however, shook her head continually. "Are you sure it was our University?"

"That is our information, yes." More head shaking. "Well, our records do go back to 1960 which is amazing, and if she was in the last year of a five-year course in 1965, she should be listed in the 1960 entry records."

"Makes sense." I contributed, but there was more head-shaking from Ms Lemon, coupled now with a look of forlorn frustration.

"Well," she said suddenly, her eyes open wide. "We did not have a Dianne Holland, archaeology student in 1965.

The course of 1960 shows only two students listed as archaeology students."

My heart sank. A wasted journey.

"One was Mr A.J.Needham, from Durham. The other, a Ms D Greenway," she looked up with a puzzled look, "but next to that name in brackets is Holland."

It took me a few seconds to comprehend the significance of that statement. "You mean she had two names?" I asked.

Ms Lemon looked at the screen again. "It looks like she applied under the name Greenway back in 1959 when she expected to qualify for entrance but changed her name to Holland on arrival. "Perhaps she married," she added as if that was a logical explanation.

"I don't think they would have allowed married students back in those days, do you?" I suggested.

"I guess not," she replied, somewhat sourly, "but what other explanation could there be?"

We sat staring at each other for a few moments. "Do you have any other information on Ms Greenway," I asked.

She looked back at the screen. "Yes, I have an address. It's in Ireland. I'll print it out for you," adding, "So, do you think this is the same person?"

"It could be, but I won't know until we make further enquiries. Thank you very much for your help."

Her face blushed, and she smiled gently. She handed me the A4 sheet headed 1960 Archaeology, Year One. It was sparse with information but did confirm the name Dianne Greenway, (Holland) plus an address in Cobh, Co.Cork, Ireland. I could already hear Jayne remonstrating about leaving her.

On the train back to London, I called Jonathan with the new information so he could start to investigate.

It had been a worthwhile journey, after all, assuming, of course, this was the same person, but something inside me kept saying I was on the right track.

One question however I kept asking myself was should I tell Michael Parker this new information. He knows her as one name, so would it do any harm to keep that memory? I decided not to call him just now, but wait until I had heard from Jonathan, and had my meeting with Morris on Monday. Tomorrow was Friday, so depending on what the new search throws up I could be back at my regular job next week. Something in me was disappointed at that thought. I kept asking myself why she would lie about her name.

Then a thought struck me. "Stupid me," I said aloud. Luckily there were very few fellow passengers on the 2.30 back to London, so I did not raise too many eyebrows. Their first meeting was the British Museum. I wondered if they kept records of holiday students that far back. It was another lead, and I still had time to go there today.

I grabbed a taxi at St Pancras station hoping to get to Great Russell Street in ten minutes, but the traffic was heavy, and it took twenty-five minutes, arriving at 4.30pm. I had an hour before the museum closed and to discover the offices, and who to talk to.

I headed to the nearest information desk. There were two people in front of me and only one person behind the desk. I was feeling impatient, which was unusual for me as I am not that sort of person. I am described by my mother as quiet and studious whenever she volunteers information about me, but for some reason today I was feeling anxious.

Now just one person in front of me.

"Come on, come on," I repeated under my breath. The clock above the desk showed 4.45pm. Come on, come on."

I must have mumbled too loudly that time as the guy in front turned around and gave me a stare. I smiled. It usually works.

At last. "I need to see someone in recruitment or HR regarding someone who worked here back in around 1965."

The lady, Jean, according to her name badge, looked at me blankly. "I don't know we would have that information here," she said slowly, thinking all the time if I was a time-waster or not.

"Would someone in HR be of help perhaps?" I prompted again, and she picked up the phone on the desk and pressed a number.

"Simon, I have a gentleman here wanting to look at our personnel records. He's from a solicitor's office trying to find someone who worked here in 1965." There was a pause. "Yes, I know, that's what I said. Could you come and see him . . . yes . . . yes . . . thank you, Simon."

"Our Mr Briggs will be down to see you. If you could wait over there," and pointed to a space away from her little domain.

"Thank you for your help," I said, as pleasantly as possible.

I hadn't been here for ages, and looking around the impressive entrance wondered why. The white rotund library, with its two sweeping staircases dominates the main entrance. This is offset on each side by large Palladian facades leading to exhibits from all over the world. The museum of 1965 would have been much different. Much darker and quieter than now.

Museums today encourage people, especially the young, to "interact" by using all of the senses, making the learning experience far more enjoyable. Lost in the literature I was reading about the current events, I did not notice Simon Briggs approaching me.

"Are you the solicitor?" he asked.

"Yes," I confirmed, offering my hand, and passing him my card. He studied this for a moment and asked what it was I wanted. I explained the situation as I had done to the helpful Ms Lemon in Leicester, hoping for the same degree of success. Most of the time he kept studying my business card, not wanting to make eye contact.

When I had finished my story he finally looked at me. "I am not sure we have records that far back, and even if we did I am not sure any casual workers would be recorded if they were only here on work experience," and gave an anxious smile.

"OK, I understand it's a long shot, but any information you find would be of benefit to the lady in question." I took the card back and wrote Dianne Holland on the back."

There was no reason to suspect she would give another name here if she were using it at the Uni.

Handing it back I said, "Please see what you can find out and call me or email me here," pointing to my details on the card.

Thinking that was the end of our brief meeting he suddenly perked up and smiled.

"Yes . . . OK, I will see if anyone in personnel can help, but it won't be until Monday."

"That's fine, any time soon would be great." We shook hands and parted company.

I stood there for a moment longer taking in the atmosphere, and wishing I had time to go through one of those imposing stone doorways into another world.

Maybe Jayne and I could come back on Sunday.

Jonathan hadn't called me back by the time I got home so I called his mobile. "Hey, any news friend."

"Well . . ." he wanted to keep me in suspense.

"Come on," I grunted.

"OK, it's like this. Your Dianne Holland is not in the system in the UK or Ireland."

"What!" I almost shouted into the phone. "How can that be? Are you saying she is not British or Irish?"

"Hang on my friend," he interrupted. I then searched for Dianne Greenway, and hey-presto, we had a match in Ireland. Co. Cork to be precise, the same address you gave me."

"That's great. So she did change names, assuming she is our girl, and that ties in with the Uni info." I said, now sounding more excited at having a solid lead. "But why use a different name?"

"There is one possibility," Jonathan offered, "she was adopted. I've come across it before when searching for relatives."

"Yes," I said slowly, trying to understand the implication.

"Are you still there?"

"Sorry, yes, just thinking. So what do we need to do now?" I asked.

"I can check adoptions around that time if it was legal."

"Legal, you mean it could have been done without anyone knowing?" I butted in.

"Yes, if the family were friends, or they had an arrangement for cash . . . there are ways, and back in the forty's during the war, paperwork may not have been as meticulous as it is today."

Too many angles were racing through my head. From not having any idea who this lady is, to finding out her real name, and that she could have been adopted, or not.

"OK, Jonathan, can you check adoption records around 1940 – 1945 in Ireland, and the electoral role in Co. Cork?"

"Is that all!" He choked.

"Well, if you can tell me were Dianne Greenway/Holland is, that would help a lot."

"That's your job. Leave the rest with me, but you may want to pack a bag for a trip to Ireland."

. . .

Back in the office, my desk had been taken over by my colleague Raj, another trainee clerk, who has been with the firm for six months.

"How's it going, Raj?" I asked, looking at the pile of files in my IN TRAY.

He looked up with a smile. "Thank God you are back. The workload is getting crazy."

"Sorry to disappoint, but I have not finished my . . ." and found it hard to describe what it was I was doing just then. The word quest had been used, but mission was probably more accurate, ". . . mission."

His face dropped. "Some buggers get all the good jobs, swanning around all over."

"It's not that glamorous I assure you. Mostly searching old files, and spending hours on the web." Even if that was massaging the truth, it should reassure him I was not on a jolly.

I promised to look over some files he was having problems with before I left, and suggested he put all the IN TRAY files into stacks, depending on their urgency. That will keep him busy for a while.

I set-up shop in the boardroom. The first email was from Michael Parker.

"Hello, James. Just a line to see if any progress. I know you said you would report back next week, but waiting is not my strongest quality or luxury just now.

Kind regards, Michael"

Damn. I didn't want to raise his hopes, but on the other hand . . . well, he started knowing nothing, so the status-quo could remain for the time being.

"Dear Mr Parker I have nothing concrete to report just now but I have several lines of enquiry I am following and should be able to report back to you early next week.

Regards, James Lacey"

Still nothing from Jonathan. Was that good or bad? I took out my notebook and added all the information gathered so far.

* Dianne Greenway/Holland. Went to Leicester Uni   1960 aged 18 (?) used the name Holland.
* Home address: 456 Russell Heights, Cobh, Cork.
* May have been adopted

I was mildly pleased with what I had, considering I started with nothing.

The boardroom door opened. It was Mr Morris, who got straight to the point – no pleasantries. "So, James, what have you to report?" he asked taking a chair opposite me.

"I thought we were to meet on Monday, sir."

"Yes . . . but I promised to see what the situation is as of now," he trailed off sounding hesitant.

It was obvious Michael Parker had either called him or emailed him in the past ten minutes since he got my reply.

"I have emailed Mr Parker this morning advising him I will contact him Monday with an update. I do not have all the information back yet from Frasier & Frasier."

Morris considered this for a moment. "OK, I'll put him off until Monday, but you had better have a report on my desk first thing." And he was gone.

No pressure then. Where the hell was Jonathan? I sent him an email.

He replied with one word. "Patience."

I busied myself helping Raj for a couple of hours until my mobile vibrated. It was a text from Jonathan.

"Meet for lunch. Churchill at 1."

Why can't we have a proper meeting in an office, not the local pub, in this case, The Churchill Arms in Kensington Church Street? I arrived at 12.45 to ensure I reserved a table as this place was packed by one o'clock on a Friday.

It's probably one of the oldest pubs in London and is a favorite with locals and tourists alike who flock here not just for the beer, but for the fantastic Thai food. Jonathan arrived within five minutes. "Not got them in yet," he complained.

"No, I'm saving our seats. Which is more important?"

'Touché. Orange juice I assume for you."

"No, as its Friday you can make it a bitter-shandy."

"Good God man, sacrilege." But he didn't pursue it.

Once settled and beer sampled, he opened the laptop. "Now, you are going to love me," and gave me a wicked smile.

"Cut the suspense man. What am I going to regret now?"

He sipped more beer, prolonging the agony.

"I'll pour that over you in a minute." I threatened.

"OK, are you ready for this?

Dianne Greenway, born Dianne Holland, between 12th and 15th April 1943 between Ireland and Canada, on the ocean liner Princess Ora."

I could not believe my ears. How on earth had he found all this out? I was dumbstruck.

Another sip of beer and he continued. "The Princess Ora was transporting refugees to Canada to escape the War but was attacked on 16th April mid-Atlantic.

Dianne was just a few days old and six weeks premature. Most survivors were rescued by a Royal Naval protection vessel and returned to Ireland. However, Mr & Mrs Holland died on the Ora, and little Dianne was taken by Petty Officer Greenway back to his home in Cove. That's how it's pronounced by the way. No one knows if the Greenway's gave her the name Dianne, or if she was given it by her birth mother, any such documents would have been lost at sea when the Ora finally sunk two days after the attack." He sat back in his chair looking very satisfied with himself. "Can we eat now?"

"Eat! How can you ask that after what you have just told me? It's incredible. How do you know all this?"

"Ah, well, it helps to have friends in the same game. I know this rather charming Irish lass in Dublin who works at the City Pensions office, and she likes to do me a favor now and then."

"I am not going to ask what . . . you will only brag." I said, not wanting him to get side-tracked.

"I gave her the name and town we had from the Uni info, and she was able to track the life and times of Mr & Mrs Shamus Greenway, deceased. He died in 1982, and she a year later. Now the interesting bit."

"What!" I exclaimed, "Could be more interesting than that?"

"Well, I shall tell you, dear friend," he said looking very smug. "There was another daughter, Sinead. Their Will left everything between one Dianne Greenway and her sister Sinead Greenway. Dianne was never traced, so as far as we know the sister ended up with everything."

I stared in disbelieve. "You mean she either didn't want it . . ."

". . . or she could not be found." Jonathan finished my sentence with a wide grin of self-satisfaction. "Your round I think," he said, hoping for a liquid reward.

Chapter Six

Back at the flat, I studied the information before me, ready to write a report for Morris on Monday morning. That meant writing it over the weekend which would annoy Jayne. She tries to keep work separate from home life, especially at weekends. Try telling that to a solicitor, or a teacher, or a politician.

My main concern, however, was not the report, but how to break the news to Jayne I will need to go to Ireland. Dianne Greenway grew up there, went to school there, so she must have had friends. If Cobh is a small town I am sure someone knows a secret or two, especially with the sudden appearance of a week old baby.

Jayne looked at me suspiciously. "What have you done?" she asked, watching me peeling the potatoes at the kitchen sink. "Just helping with dinner. What's wrong with that?"

"Call me suspicious . . . but you only cook during the week if you want something," and she put her arms around my waist, and slowly squeezed.

"That's not fair, and that hurts . . ." I squealed. She loosened her grip only to reapply it around my neck, and I felt her nails stroke my skin.

"Hey, that hurts too!" I said, dropping the potatoes and turning around to face her, putting my arms around her waist.

"We don't have to fight, do we? It's no big deal," and went to kiss her, but she pulled back.

"What's not a big deal, James?" she asked, looking decidedly apprehensive.

"Well, you know we said we should have a weekend break sometime . ."

Her eyes brighten and she relaxed her grip from my neck. "Oh, James, yes, York . . . no Edinburgh would be good. We could get the . . ." then she saw I was not responding. "Oh, you have somewhere in mind, don't you?"

I held her hands firmly, mainly to protect my neck and other exposed parts of my body. "How about Ireland?" and smiled one of the most sincere smiles I could muster.

She prized her hands free and I saw her knuckles were red, as were her cheeks.

"This is to do with that old man's women, isn't it?" she said, raising her voice.

"What's wrong with mixing business and pleasure, especially pleasure . . . in a lovely old Irish hotel overlooking the sea. Isn't that romantic?" I winced.

She took a deep breath and slowly shook her head. "Are you sure you haven't any Irish in you, with all that Blarney. I think you must have, James Lacey."

"Not that I know of, but we can always ask the Blarney stone when we get there," I said, sensing I had overcome the first hurdle. The second hurdle – yes that could be a little trickier. "OK, now one more thing, my love . . ."

"Oh, no . . . my love . . . What else is there?"

"Well, it's more a mid-week break than a weekend break. Preferably next Wednesday and Thursday." And waited for the torrent of verbal abuse, but it didn't come, much to my surprise. "How about a neck break?" She came closer and put her hands around my throat again and pretended to choke me. At least I think she pretended.

It cost me dinner Saturday evening and a very expensive bottle of wine. Funny how women feel they must get back something in return for giving in. I spent Sunday drafting my report and eventually finished it around 6.00pm.

Jayne had been on the phone several times to colleagues trying to juggle appointments, and finally confirmed she had rearranged her week to accommodate our trip.

Having kissed and made-up, again, I logged on to book a flight to Cork. "Wednesday, returning Thursday evening," I announced.

"Call that a weekend break, James? I have just rearranged my workload for Wednesday, Thursday and Friday. If we are going that far it's got to be worthwhile."

"Jayne, be reasonable. I've got to report back on Friday."

"You can prepare your report on the plane on the way home. I am sure you will be taking your laptop," she suggested, and with a certain tone that was non-negotiable.

So I booked us three nights in Cobh at the Commodore Hotel. In hindsight, maybe an extra day would be an advantage in case I have to track down friends or relations. At least that should pacify Morris.

I got into the office Monday morning at 8.45am and sat at my desk wondering what Raj had done with the mountain of files I last saw here. I was about to look through some of the leftover files when Mr Morris put his head around the door. "Ah, good. Come on in James so we can talk over what you have so far."

I sat at the wide desk, covered in papers and files, and placed my report in the only available space I could see.

Morris picked it up and started to read it. "This looks very thorough James," noticing the report was probably thicker than he had expected. "Run through the salient points while I read."

I started with what he already knew and progressed to   the finding of the name Greenway at the University, and   the subsequent discovery of the possible adoption by the Greenway's after the death of Dianne's parents in the Atlantic, "and I must say how helpful Frasier & Frasier have been."

Morris looked up from reading. "Your lunchtime meetings with your friend have been rewarding then," he said coldly.

I winced. "Err, yes, I believe they have, sir." And left it at that, remembering to tell Jonathan he owes me now.

"This is amazing. To think a simple search for a missing person could result in all of this drama." He shook his head and looked at me again. "So, James, what do you propose to tell Mr Parker?"

I had been prepared for that. The last thing I wanted to be was for Morris to call Michael Parker and fill him in on what we . . . I have.

"Well, sir, I need to confirm the Irish connection. I know Mr & Mrs Greenway are deceased, but they must have had relatives, and the sister may still be alive. Dianne must have grown up with school friends. I plan to visit Cobh this week and will report back next Monday to Mr Parker on my findings. I don't think we need to tell him everything just yet, do we sir?"

Morris looked at me in such a way I thought he was going to pick holes in my argument. "Hmm, OK, but keep the trip short and keep all expense receipts. When are you leaving?"

Damn. I was hoping he wouldn't ask me that. "Mid-week sir. I'll help Raj out until then," and got up to leave.

"James." I froze at the door.

"Sir"

"Don't go turning over too many rocks. Small communities can resent outsiders."

"I'll do my best, sir," and made my exit.

It felt strange tackling my usual work for a couple of days, and my heart wasn't really in it. I could only keep thinking about Dianne Greenway, and where she could be. Funny though, I never thought for a moment she may be dead.

The flight to Cork was smooth, and we landed at 11.30am. By the time we sorted out a hire car and found the Commodore Hotel it was nearer 1.0pm. I wanted to get out there and start investigating, but Jayne had other ideas. After we unpacked and changed, she wanted to check out the pool and spa. "I've booked us a massage each at 6.00 o'clock, my treat," she informed me.

"But I've never had a massage."

"Then it's about time you experienced one," and looked me in the eyes the way she does, and put her arms around my neck and pulled me closer. "Now, James, what can we do for the next few hours?"

Next morning we agreed to go our separate ways. Jayne got a taxi and went shopping in Cork, and I went investigating. The only lead I had was the Greenway's old address in Russell Heights. Cobh is a small town, and if I had known it better I could have walked for twenty minutes, but I drove there, following the directions the receptionist had given me.

The area lived up to its name. It was the highest point in the town, with spectacular views overlooking the harbor, and the Irish Sea beyond. The "Heights" as it is known locally, was a very different place sixty years ago. Most, if not all, were terraced council houses; small and uniform in design and aesthetics. The area is divided into four housing sections, with large grassy areas and walkways and benches between them. Most houses now are privately owned and seem to have been transformed by the owners to be as individualistic as possible. Virtually all were painted a different color; yellow, blue, red, green, salmon pink, cool grey, and a few brilliant whites.

Some even looked new built, and there were several properties where some of the smaller terraced houses had been made into one larger house.

Cobh has had its share of misery and misfortune over the centuries, but now, as a tourist town, its fortunes have been transformed, and the good people of Cobh are seeing the rewards.

Having slowly circumnavigated the area, I found number 456. It was at the end of a terrace, tucked snugly against a walled area, beyond which was the garden of a larger property. 456 was painted a warm cream, and as with all these houses seemed it was only done recently.

I sat in the car going over what I would say. The chances of the present owners knowing the Greenways were remote, but I had to start somewhere. The bell rang. A dog barked. I stepped back from the porch. The door was opened by an elderly lady with neat silver hair, and sparkling blue eyes. Her first thoughts were that I was selling something, double glazing or home insurance. "We're fine, thank you," she said clearly, in a wonderful soft Irish accent. I was so taken by her blue eyes I almost forgot why I was there. "Sorry," I stuttered. "I am not selling anything. My name is James Lacey. I am a solicitor from London, looking for information on someone who lived here many years ago."

"Who would that be then?" she asked.

"Mr and Mrs Shamus Greenway. Do you know the name?" She just looked blank at first, and I was prepared to leave when she answered. "I should do. They were my parents."

This was Sinead Greenway, Dianne's sister, the eighty-year-old daughter of the Greenways. She invited me in.

"Will you have tea?" she asked politely in her lovely soft accent. I think she would have made it even if I had said no. "Now sit down and tell me why you want to know about my parents."

She studied me while sipping her tea. "You are not dressed like solicitors I knew. Everyone is casual these days I suppose," she said with a look of remembering. It was true, I was in casual clothes. I had not thought about wearing a suit over here. I did have a business card which I hoped would reassure her.

"I am sorry, you are correct. I am over here on business and pleasure. I'm here with my girlfriend for a couple of days sightseeing, so I thought I would take the opportunity to check out your parents."

She looked at me curiously. "And why do you need to do that after all these years."

I was feeling a little nervous now and I was not sure how she would react to my searching questions. But I was about to find out. "I am trying to find anything I can on Dianne Holland . . . or Dianne Greenway as you know her, your sister."

On hearing that name she nearly dropped her cup and saucer. I quickly jumped up and rescued it before it stained the carpet.

Her cheeks turned blue and she was breathing heavier. "Are you OK?" I asked. "Can I get you something?" She pointed to a small tin on the coffee table next to the teapot.

I picked it up and opened it. Her hands were shaking so much she could not make contact with the small pills. I took a few out and placed them on my palm. She tried to smile but concentrated on picking up a tablet from my hand and swallowing it, then another. "Do you want some water?"

I asked. She shook her head and leant back in the armchair, looking exhausted.

All I could think was, 'thank goodness she is OK.' I could imagine the situation if I had to call an ambulance, and explain why I was there, alone in this old lady's house – a stranger from England, or from wherever they thought I was from, having seen my Asian complexion.

After a few minutes, her breathing was calmer and she managed to lift the teacup without spilling it. "You had me worried there for a moment," I said, but she did not respond. She looked away from me, looking up and then sideways, as if hoping to see something, or someone, familiar.

"I am sorry if I upset you, Ms Greenway," I said quietly, and as reassuringly as possible.

Then still without making eye contact, she said, "I want you to leave now," and she closed her eyes tightly.

I realized I couldn't upset her further, so I wrote my mobile phone number on my card and left it on the coffee table, hoping she may reconsider.

Back in the car, I called Jayne. "Hope you haven't spent all our Euros."

"Of course not silly. I paid by credit card," she said, happy with herself, while I pondered the logic of that reply.

"How are you getting on with your search? Find any old skeletons?"

"Well, I did find a relative of the Greenway's," a daughter, but as soon as I mentioned Dianne she almost had a heart attack, and asked me to leave."

"What are you going to do then?"

"Let's meet back at the hotel for lunch and decide then, that's if you have finished shopping."

"Don't be silly, James . . . a girl is never finished shopping."

We had a light lunch in the Commodore Bar while planning the rest of the day.

"Personally, I think we should have a siesta," Jayne whispered in my ear. "All that shopping can tire a girl out," she said with her most alluring come to bed eyes.

"Stop it," I said, without thinking straight. "I need to know more from Sinead Greenway. And why hasn't Jonathan called back?" I asked, dialing his number.

"Jonathan, I can hardly hear you," I said loudly. Jayne tapped my arm and put a finger to her lips to tell me to stop shouting. I walked outside the bar where I could hear clearer.

"Is that you, James, how's the Guinness?"

"Don't like it. Listen. I found the daughter. Sinead Greenway. She's still living at the same address, but she didn't want to talk about her sister."

"So, more time to spend in the bar. Sounds a good plan."

"Be serious. I need to know anything you can find out about her. Can your friend help? The one in Dublin."

"I'll give her a call and see what I can find out. Love to Jayne."

"So, what did Johnny boy have to say?" she asked pouring me another glass of red wine.

"Hey, no more. I need a clear head."

"What for? Who else do you have to see now you have lost your best lead?" She said with an air of sarcasm.

She was right. Where indeed could I go? Sinead could have answered so many questions – and still can. "That's it. We have to go back and talk to her."

"We! Don't you mean you have to go back?"

"No, love. I need you with me for reassurance. If she sees us together I think she may open up. Will you come?"

We got back to Sinead's house around 3.00pm. "This is nice," Jayne commented, seeing the painted houses. "Very neat."

We stood at the door and I took a deep breath. I rang the bell. A dog barked. "She must be out," I said after a couple of minutes.

"I don't think so, not unless curtains move by themselves." Jayne nodded to the window on our right.

One last attempt. I opened the letterbox and called out. "Ms Greenway, Sinead, I've come back with my girlfriend. We just want to talk. Please, just a few moments." I said with a hint of desperation.

The door slowly opened but was on the chain this time. "I don't want to talk about my sister," she said firmly.

I was about to plead again when Jayne stood next to me. "Hello, Sinead, my name is Jayne. You have a lovely house. I bet the views over the sea are wonderful."

Sinead looked at Jayne and must have seen something of herself in her. Whatever it was, she released the chain and opened the door. "OK, come on in for a minute as you are here."

I frowned but said nothing. Jayne turned to me and poked out her tongue. I stood in the front room I had been in a few hours earlier, but this time noticed several photographs on the mantelpiece. One old black and white of an elderly couple, Shamus and his wife. Then another of Shamus on his own in Merchant Seaman uniform. He looked proud and handsome.

Other photos slowly revealed more people. Sinead for sure, but one with a man and a young woman. Her daughter maybe?

Just then Jayne came in from the kitchen carrying a tray of tea. "Glad I brought you along." I joked.

"Sinead and I have been having a great chat. The view out back is wonderful James. You should take a look before we go."

Jayne sat next to Sinead on the two-seater sofa, and I sat opposite in the armchair. They looked like mother and daughter, and I felt I was being interviewed.

"So, James, where are you from?" Sinead asked, avoiding the reason we were there.

"London, Acton actually, West London," I replied.

"No, where are you from, your family etc. . ." She repeated. I haven't been asked that since University. "Originally my Grandparents came from India in 1946 just before partition. We still have relatives in Kerala." How much more did she want to know for goodness sake? I want to be the one asking questions here.

"Ah, relatives. We all have them. Mores' the pity sometimes," she said bitterly. Then her eyes widened and she looked directly at me. "OK, ask me what you want to know, but I cannot promise to answer all of them."

I looked at Jayne who was sitting demurely and sipping tea.

"We have been asked by a client to see if Dianne Holland . . . Greenway, is still alive, and where she is living. That's the essence of our visit. What can you tell us about her, and why did she change her name back to Holland?"

Sinead looked down at her intertwined bony fidgeting fingers. Jayne placed a hand on hers. "If it's too painful we can come back," she offered with a gentle smile. She was good, very good.

"No, I'm fine my dear. I'll tell you what you want to know, but one thing, I have no idea where she is now if she is dead or alive even," her face was still. Eyes just staring into nowhere.

My heart sank, but I wanted to hear the full story.

"My father, Shamus, was a Petty Officer on the Princess Ora when it was attacked in the Atlantic in 1943.

A passenger, Mrs Judith Holland, had given birth on-board before the attack, but both she and her husband died in the battle. My father rescued the baby and brought her back to Cobh. I was five years old and thought my mother had given birth to a baby sister. We grew up as sisters and everything was wonderful," she paused to remember, just as Michael Parker had done.

"Your parents did register her to the authorities then?" I asked.

"I don't know. Or didn't know then of course. I was a child, we were sisters was all I knew."

Jayne was still holding her hands, which Sinead seemed to appreciate.

"We went to the same school, St. Aloysius in Cork. We took the bus every day there and back. We did everything together. Shared clothes. Liked the same pop music. Went to the Youth Club on Lake Road every Friday, and ate fish and chips on the way home."

Another pause. This time her expression changed. She looked somber. I was about to ask if she wanted to go on, but Jayne shook her head and patted her hand, and Sinead continued.

"She was a clever girl. Far cleverer than me. She had ambitions to go to University and to travel the world. I suppose it was seeing dad go off so many times, and hearing his stories she wanted it for herself." She suddenly stood up and picked up the photo of Shamus in his merchant seaman uniform. Sitting down again she showed it to Jayne. "He was handsome," Jayne said.

"Yes, he was," she answered with a glint of a tear in her eye.

"Didn't you want to go to University Sinead?" Jayne asked.

"No, not me. I wasn't that clever. I wanted to leave school and work in a shop. I did leave school at fifteen, but Dianne went on to sixth form, and eventually enrolled to . . . Leicester I think it was."

"Yes, Leicester, to study Archaeology," I confirmed.

"Well, that's when my world fell apart. When she was eighteen, just before she was to leave, mum and dad told her the truth about her parents, that she was adopted."

"What happened then?" I asked with interest.

She sighed deeply. "Dianne snapped. She could not believe what she was hearing. She kept shouting "It's a lie" and "why do you hate me?" She thought it was to keep her from going to University, but that was already arranged. Dad was depressed for days. They hardly spoke to each other before she left. Not even me. She thought I knew all along, which was ridiculous, just because . . ." and then she stopped, and the tears came. My phone rang and broke the silence. It was Jonathan.

"Hey, James, you'll never guess . . ."

I walked into the kitchen to take the call and stood half-listening to Jonathan and half looking at the view Jayne had described. It was indeed a lovely view and understood why Sinead may never have wanted to leave here. On the windowsill was a framed photo of a young girl. Not the same one as in the other picture. This child was about four or five years old, holding a beach ball in the garden. She looked happy, but at the same time, distant.

I sat back in the armchair looking too serious. "What's up, James?" Jayne asked.

I looked at Sinead, who was still red-eyed, and leant forward slightly "Just because of what, Sinead?" I asked gently.

Jayne looked confused and gave me one of her silent looks.

". . . because I was adopted as well," she eventually answered, confirming what Jonathan had just told me.

We sat in silence, not knowing what to say next. But Sinead knew we wanted to hear her out.

"My mum and dad told me on my eighteenth birthday as well, five-year before. I had taken the news rather differently, and Dianne wasn't told for a few weeks later. However, I accepted my fate.

My real mother had died in childbirth, and my father was unknown, so I was put in an orphanage where my parents found me. Mother worked at the orphanage so she saw who came and went." She was talking more fluidly now and seemed at ease with the recollections.

"Anyway, I knew my place was here, but Dianne went to English school, and we didn't see her for nearly three years."

"She came back then. When was this?" I asked eagerly

"Oh, I'm not sure of the dates now, but she had not come back to make amends. She came to say goodbye forever. She was going to travel, then go back to University and then . . . I don't know . . . somewhere exotic," and shrugged her shoulders.

I still felt she was holding something back. She wasn't making eye contact, and kept fidgeting, and staring at the ceiling or the mantelpiece . . . yes, the photos.

"May I ask who is that is with you in one of the photos?" I gestured to the mantelpiece.

She looked with sadness and I felt bad at asking. "That was a long time ago. We never married. That was his daughter. He had separated, but his wife would not divorce him, so we could never marry. Those days were different then," and she touched the frame with fondness. "He died back in 1979 and his daughter went her own way. I never saw her again either."

I let her reminisce a while longer.

"Sinead." I got her to look at me. "Was Dianne pregnant when you last saw her?" I asked, looking directly at her.

She gave a puzzled look and turned to Jayne. She was trying to speak but no words came. She was also shaking a little. Jayne put a hand on her shoulders and rubbed her gently. I remembered the tablets and looked for the small tin.

"It's OK," Jayne said quietly and reassuringly, "we will leave you alone now."

I, however, did not want to leave and shot her a look, which she ignored. I wanted to know the answer to my question.

Sinead went to stand, and Jayne helped her to balance, and she didn't object to Jayne holding her arm as she walked into the kitchen.

A few moments later they returned. Sinead was holding the photo I had seen in the kitchen of the young girl.

Her hand was still shaking as she handed it to me. "This is the only photo I have of Kimberly. Taken just before Dianne took her back."

Jayne eased her back onto the sofa, but she was still shaking slightly, and breathing faster. I went and fetched a glass of water. "Here, have some of this Sinead," I said holding the glass while she drank.

"Thank you," she managed. "I haven't talked to anyone before, in or out of the family about what happened. It was what she wanted."

I looked at Jayne briefly, but I didn't want to lose eye contact with Sinead now she was talking, so I sat back on the edge of my chair waiting for her to continue.

"Well, to answer your question, no, she was not pregnant on that occasion. It was a year later she came home again, after University, or towards the end, I can't really remember."

"You are doing just fine," Jayne said, patting her hand. "So how far pregnant was she then?"

"Around three months I think," she said, blinking.

"Can you remember the month by any chance?" I wanted to know.

"Yes, I can. It was the end of August, in 1965. The leanbh was born in March 1966, two weeks late. She called her Kimberly, and she was a darling wee leanbh," she said with a faint smile.

Michael Parker was right. She had left him because she was pregnant - but where are mother and daughter now?

"Sinead, did she ever say who the father was?" I asked gently.

"No," she shrugged "One of those hippies' from where she was in England, we thought, but she never said."

"What did your parents say or do. Did they support her?" I asked.

Again, Sinead closed her eyes and breathed deeply. Was she trying to block it out, or trying to remember? She reached for a tissue tucked in her cardigan sleeve, but just played with it.

"Dianne didn't want the child at first. She was twenty-four and she had her life planned out. She wanted to travel the world, doing what she had studied for."

"She could have had an abortion in London. That would have solved everything" I said, hoping not to sound too matter-of-fact.

"I suppose she could have. Some of that Catholic school upbringing must have rubbed off on to her." And she gave a tentative smile.

Keeping the slightly lighter mood going I said, "I know of a song lyric that talks about Catholic girls being . . ." but Jayne had other ideas. "James . . . not now," she said with a piercing glare . . . "I don't think Sinead wants to hear your song trivia," and turned back to Sinead. "Go on, please. You are doing fine my dear."

"Well, after the birth she stayed for three months to feed her, and then left to go back to London."

"London!" I repeated. "Then she could have." but thought better of it. "Sorry. Just thinking out loud."

Sinead looked at me blankly. "She went to London for two years I think, then to Paris," she took a sip of water before continuing.

"Did she want you to adopt the child to bring her up as your own?" Jayne asked.

"Well, you would have thought so, but she didn't. She did not want her to go through what we had . . . being told on her eighteenth birthday she was adopted.

You see, Dianne had not forgiven mum and dad for that, but she knew they would look after her. She wrote often, and sent money when she could," she paused again, but I was eager to hear the end, as far as Sinead knew it. I had questions swimming around my mind, and wanted to call Jonathan, but decided to wait until I had heard more.

This was turning into something far more than I had expected, and I was literally on the edge of the chair, wanting to hear her out.

So, when did she take . . . Kimberly was it?"

"Dianne suddenly reappeared in 1970. The child was nearly four years old. She stayed three weeks so they got to know each other some more, then left . . . one Spring morning, on the 15th March . . ." and her voice trailed off, remembering that day. Sinead would have been thirty-one years old, and women back then hardly ever had children at that age. By then she had resigned herself to spinsterhood, and to a life of looking after her parents in their old age. She might even have secretly despised her sister for leaving her alone to look after their parents, or even envied her boldness to leave Cobh, and start a new life.

"I think we should go now, James. Sinead needs a rest." Jayne said, about to stand up, but Sinead held on to her hand. "No, it's fine my dear. I'm OK, really," she said rather unconvincingly.

"I have so many questions, but Jayne is right. We can come back tomorrow if you are OK with that."

"I don't think there is a lot more to say really." Then she added "What will happen when . . . if, you find her?" she asked with some interest.

"I have a letter to give her. That is all," and smiled, I hope, reassuringly.

Jayne finally stood to go. "Two questions, if I may before we go. Can you remember anything particularly . . . interesting about her? Something only you may know."

Sinead stood up and held Jayne's arm. "No, not really. Only . . . she did like tea . . . drank nothing else.

They called her the tea lady at school . . ." And then her thoughts trailed off again. "What was the other question?" she suddenly asked.

"Your parents Will. Did they leave everything to you?"

Sinead blinked several times as if trying to focus. "No, in fact, they left everything to be split between the two of us, even after the way she treated them, they still wanted her to have a share. When you first came and said you were a solicitor I thought she had wanted to finally claim her share. We did try to find her but to this day her part of the Will is still unclaimed. When I pass over, I have left it all to her. I never married of course and we have no other relations."

As we walked to the front door Sinead suddenly said, "I won't be a moment." We saw her go into the kitchen. I shrugged at Jayne and blew her a kiss.

Sinead re-appeared holding some postcards. "I don't know why I kept these. Something to remember her by I suppose. I don't know why she sent them. Guilt maybe. Here, take them. They may be of some use." And she handed me half a dozen unwritten postcards from all over the world.

"Thank you, Sinead. I know how hard this has been for you. If I do find Dianne alive and well, I will persuade her to come and visit, I promise." Easier said than done, but I did mean it.

We said our goodbyes. Jayne gave her a hug and a kiss, and we promised to look in on her before we left for the airport on Saturday.

We sat in the car reflecting on what we had just heard. "Wow, both adopted," I said, "and the child. Michael Parker will be . . ." what, I thought.

Delighted. Happy. Elated. Overjoyed. "How do you think old man Parker will react to the news that he has a daughter?"

Jayne just shrugged. "It's want he wanted to know wasn't it? So tell him, and get back to a proper job," she said poking me in the ribs. She went back to looking at the postcards I had given her to hold. They were from all over the world; Paris, Cairo, India, Greece.

"She is a sweet old lady. It's a shame we had to stir up all those memories." Jayne said sadly.

I looked at her and smiled. "You were great. She would never have opened up like that if you had not been there." And I leant over and gave her kiss on the cheek.

"As a reward then," she turned to me and smiled, "can we go back to the hotel and have that siesta before dinner." Who was I to refuse?

The next day we decided to be tourists. After breakfast, we walked down to the seafront. The sun was shining and the sky was blue. We strolled along the harbor and took photos of expensive sailing boats, and gulls swooping for fish and scraps of leftover fast food. Further along Westbourne Place, we came across the Sirius Art Gallery. Jayne wasn't too keen, but we looked in. I was fascinated by a photographic exhibition of shorebirds, while Jayne perused the gift shop.

"Can't you go into a shop without buying anything?" I said in astonishment at her bag of purchases. "Don't be mean, otherwise you may not get your present," she teased.

It was a book of bird photography I had been looking at in the exhibition. "Thank you. It's wonderful." I said sincerely, wishing I had thought of buying her something as well.

There are many plaques and memorials here, but the two most looked at are probably in memory to the Titanic, which was her last port of call before that fateful voyage, and the passenger ship Lusitania, which also suffered the same fate, with heavy loss of life. Cobh was where the survivors were brought, as was one other orphan child twenty-seven years later.

Back at the hotel, we had lunch in the Quay Bar.

Jayne was studying the map when she spotted where she wanted to go. "Hey, we're only a short drive to Blarney Castle, where the famous Kissing Stone is."

I gave her a blank look. "Oh, come on, James, you must have heard of the Blarney Stone. They say if you kiss it, it brings you love, luck and happiness," she beamed.

"Don't we have those already?" I said, determined to spend a quiet afternoon walking locally or drafting my report or reading my new present.

"Come on, it's only about twenty minutes' drive. It looks lovely. Look, I got it up on my iPhone," and she thrust the screen in front of me.

"OK. OK." I surrendered. "We will go, but I am not kissing anything unless it kisses me back." I said, leaning over and giving her a gentle kiss on the lips, before adding "You know it's just a tourist grabber, like the Loch Ness Monster. It brings in the money."

"You are no fun sometimes, James Lacey," she said with more than a hint of mockery.

The drive through County Cork was wonderful. Green rolling hills with neat farmlands and country pubs. Blarney Castle was more interesting than I imagined, despite its main attraction of being held upside down to kiss a cold stone wall.

Jayne was getting in position to take her turn of the kissing ritual when my mobile rang.

"Is that Mr Lacey?" a voice with an Irish accent asked. "Yes, speaking. Who is this?"

"Mr Lacey, this is Inspector O'Callaghan from Cork Garda. Are you in Ireland Mr Lacey?"

"Yes, but why. Is anything wrong?"

"Do you know Ms Sinead Greenway living in Russell Heights? Is just that we found your solicitors card in her house. Were you there on business?"

"Yes, sort off. What's happened for you to be there? Is she OK?" I asked, but feared the answer.

"I'm afraid she died last night. A neighbor found her when she didn't come round for lunch. Seems she died in her sleep."

I held the phone to my ear but I was not listening any more. Dead! Less than twenty-four hours after we met her. All kinds of thoughts were racing through my mind. Did she find the ordeal of remembering the past too much? Did we cause it? Was she more ill than I realized?

"Hey, I hope you got a good shot of me then . . . James . . . what's up? You did take a picture didn't you . . ?"

"Mr Lacey. Are you there . . ?"

My head was spinning with voices coming at me from all angles. Jayne brought me back by hitting my shoulder. "Jayne," I said with a dazed expression. "There's been some sad news . . ." then I realized the Inspector was still on the line.

"Hello Inspector, yes I'm still here. Yes, we are at the Commodore Hotel in Cobh. We'll be back around 4.00. Yes, see you then."

"Who was that, what's happened, James?" Jayne asked, now looking as anxious as I was.

I took her arm, and we walked away from the crowds overseeing the kissing ritual.

"It's Sinead. She's dead." I finally said. Jayne looked drained of color and was looking puzzled. "Dead! How? When? She was fine yesterday when we left . . . who was on the phone?"

"The police. They found the card I left. They want to interview us at the hotel. It's just a formality." I added, hoping to reassure her there was nothing to worry about. Old people do die. "She was in her eighties," I said. "It was her time."

Jayne looked at me through sad eyes, and a tear trickled down one cheek. "Did we do it, James? All those questions . . . all those unpleasant memories."

"Hey, look at me," I said wiping away the tear. "As I said, she was old and was taking tablets for something. It's just an unfortunate coincidence." She tried to smile but without conviction, and we hugged each other, never wanting to let go.

We drove in silence back to the hotel to meet Inspector Aidan O'Callaghan who was accompanied by two uniformed Garda. We sat in the corner of the resident's lounge, which, thankfully, was not occupied.

"Thank you for seeing me, Mr Lacey. Can you tell me why you visited Ms Greenway yesterday?"

I retold the story of how we came to be here and the conversation we had had with Sinead yesterday. All the time Jayne was holding my hand.

"You say you visited her in the morning but returned later in the day with Ms Wood. Why was that?"

"Sinead . . . Ms. Greenway, did not want to talk about her sister. She was reluctant to talk to me about the past."

"So you decided to go back with Ms Wood and intimidate her."

"Hey, no!" Jayne interrupted. "That's not what happened at all. I suggested she might be more responsive if another woman was there. That's all."

"It's OK, Jayne. I am sure the inspector was not suggesting anything else." I said, looking directly at him.

He looked at his notes to avoid my glare. "We do have a witness saying they saw you leaving the house, and hugging Ms Greenway, so I guess she was not distressed when you left her."

"That's right. We parted on good terms, and promised to look in tomorrow on our way to the airport."

"Tomorrow?" the Inspector said, "that may be too early. I need a statement from you both, and I am waiting for the autopsy, which will now not be until Monday."

Jayne and I looked at each other. "Monday! That's impossible Inspector." I said with determination. "You can have our statements tonight, but we must get back to London. You have our details and my work address." He looked at each of us in turn.

"Seeing you are a solicitor, Mr Lacey, I expect you to respect the law and uphold its investigational procedures, whatever country it may be. Is that correct?

Solicitor. . . I had not confirmed I was a solicitor, but if he was under that impression, who was I to disagree. "Of course," I answered solemnly.

"OK, if you can follow us back to the station we will take your statements. You may be required to attend a Coroner's Inquest if there is one. I assume that will be in order."

"Yes, of course we will. Thank you, Inspector."

"Does that mean we can go tomorrow?" Jayne asked, still looking very concerned.

"Yes, Miss you can." And with that we followed the Inspector back to Cork police station where we each gave our statements.

On returning to the hotel a reporter was waiting for us. "I cannot say anything else I have already told the police. I suggest you ask them if you want more information." I told the young man, eager to get an angle on Sinead's death, even if there wasn't one.

We had dinner in our room to avoid unwanted inquisitors and had an early night. I held Jayne in my arms and we drifted into sleep and closer to the return home to face more questions than I had answers for.

Chapter Seven

On the flight back to London I started to draft my report for Michael Parker, but my heart wasn't in it. I had the rest of the weekend to worry about it, not now, not here with Jayne sitting at my side, still feeling guilty about Sinead's death. I kept going over and over in my mind to see if I could have changed what we asked her, or how we asked it. My conclusion was no, we couldn't. I just hope the Coroner agrees with me, if, or when, we are called to the inquest. I put my Dell Notebook back in its case and saw the postcards Sinead had given me. I took them out and studied them more carefully, laying them face up on the lap tray in front of me. Jayne, who had been dozing, saw them and leant over to examine them closer. "Where are these from?" she asked, picking up the two I hadn't yet been able to identify.

"No idea, but from the looks of them somewhere in Asia or thereabouts," was all I could suggest. "I wonder why she sent them," Jayne asked rhetorically.

"That's a very good question actually," I said, leaning over and giving her a kiss on the cheek. She smiled and laid her head on my shoulder. I continued to stare at the colorful cards in front of me, except, one was in black & white. This was the one from Paris and showed a typical Paris aerial scene of the Eiffel Tower on the left, with the straight lines of the Champs-Elysées leading directly to the Arc de Triomphe. I thought it strange how postcards had changed over the years . . . then it struck me. I hastily turned over all the cards and stared at the blank messages. "What are you looking at?" she asked half asleep.

"Look," I said pointing to the cards, "what do they tell you?"

She looked closer and blinked several times. "Nothing. There's no message at all. Just an address. The same on each one." She said, putting her head back on my shoulder hoping to return to her slumber.

"Jayne, you are missing the point. It's not the message; it's the dates they were sent."

She sat up again and looked closer. "Ruddy hell, James, of course. You can tell where she was over a given timeline."

I salvaged the white serviette my drink was on and found a pen. "OK, let's see what we have," I said excitedly as I felt the adrenaline rushing through me.

I somehow thought I was close to finding the elusive Dianne Greenway and in only a few days of searching. Michael Parker would be happy. I could get back to my work, and Jayne would be relieved I was not flying off 'all over' as she puts it.

I looked closely at the stamps and tried to decipher the dates. First was the Paris card. 12.08.70, then the one from Cairo 23.10.74. Athens, 07.04.92 Delhi 06.09.86. Rawalpindi 02.04.79 Seoul 06.06.82   I listed them on the paper napkin in chronological order;

Paris, France 12th August 1970
Cairo, Egypt 23rd October 1974
Rawalpindi, India 2nd April 1979
Seoul, South Korea 21st June 1982
Delhi, India 6th September 1986
Athens, Greece 7th April 1992

We stared at the list, expecting to see, by some miracle, the answers to all our questions. But answers did not come. Were the dates significant? Was she working at these places, or are they holiday destinations - hence the postcards.

I carefully gathered them up with the napkin and put them safely back in my laptop case. I had the rest of the weekend to analyze them, and anyway, three heads are better than two.

. . .

Jayne takes Jonathan for what he is, a large lovable flirt. She lets him flirt. It's harmless, and I know she is not attracted to him in any physical way. I only hope he knows that as well.

Jonathan arrived at 1.00pm on Sunday for lunch. It's about the only thing that would entice him away from his second home, The Crooked Billet on Wimbledon Common. He was, however, also intrigued by my account of our visit to Ireland, and what we had found there.

"My lass in Dublin is going to want a big Christmas card this year," he said with a glint in his eye.

"Do I hear you being unfaithful to me, Johnny boy?" Jayne called from the kitchen.

"Never, my dear. I'm saving myself for you for when you come to your senses and leave this globetrotting workaholic."

"Globetrotting. I don't think Ireland is quite that, and anyway, Jayne was with me," I said, in my defense, "and what's more, we would not have all of this information if Jayne had not been there." I added with a hint of pride.

"Ah, lost your charm on the ladies my boy." Jonathan quipped, which I ignored. Jayne came in from the kitchen and we took a glass of wine each. "A toast," Jonathan suggested, and he raised his glass, to friends."

Jayne followed suit, "to love," she said, looking at me lovingly.

After a moment I raised my glass to touch the others, "to fate," I said slowly.

"How romantic." Jonathan moaned, turning to Jayne. "He's really into this detective lark, isn't he?"

Jayne seemed to have ignored that remark, but as I found out later she too was worried I was getting too involved in this search for someone who may not even be alive.

"You boys be good while I finish lunch, and don't drink all the wine before we eat . . . and set the table please," she demanded on her way back to the kitchen.

Not that she had gone far. Our one-bedroom flat had a large open plan lounge and kitchen. At least it had some character. The room was L-shaped, and the kitchen was tucked out of sight if you were standing in the lounge at the far end.

We had painted the walls white and adorned them with a dozen photographic prints from exotic places, each in a different frame. We had two two-seater sofas with a large wooden coffee table between them.

At the other end of the room near the kitchen was a gate-leg folding table that sat four comfortably, six at a squeeze.

"Come on," I said to Jonathan, "make yourself useful."

"I resent that. I opened the wine, and by the way, where's my bottle of 'duty-free'"? He asked, with relish.

"Ah, as it happens we did think of you, knowing you like the unusual in musical taste. The guy at the airport shop said this was an interesting CD.

It's by a Scottish lady called Mhairi Hall." And I searched my briefcase for the present we had brought him.

"Thanks, guys, that's thoughtful and will last longer than a bottle of Irish whisky. Can I put it on?"

We laid the table as instructed, and smelt the lamb wafting in from the oven. "Smells good. I'm starving." Jonathan said, pouring more wine. "OK, fifteen minutes," Jayne confirmed and held out her empty glass. "One for the cook then."

The mellow sounds of a Gaelic piano filled the room, creating a calming and peaceful atmosphere.

"Show Johnny the post-cards, James. See what he makes of them."

"Good idea," I said, and took the six postcards with the folded napkin from my laptop case.

"Sinead gave me these as we left. From what we can make out from the post-marks, they were posted between 1970 and 1992, but why, is anyone's guess."

Jonathan looked at the cards in turn and laid them out on the coffee table in date order, as I had done on the plane. He looked at a card and then my list, then back to the cards, and back to the list. "Good, except Rawalpindi is in Pakistani, not India," he said without looking up.

"So, these could have been holiday destinations, where she was working, or just passing through," he said, still studying the cards. "But if we look at them with some lateral thinking, and few more glasses of wine, it could be possible to deduce, my dear Watson, given she was a qualified archaeologist if these are from work or pleasure," he smiled, pleased with his deduction.

"OK, Holmes, but don't play the violin. It disturbs the neighbors." I said laughing. He did have a point though.

"So what you are saying is, are these places renowned for archaeology, or as a holiday destination."

"Well, it's a start. We will need to do a lot of Googling."

". . . not until later. Lunch is served, gentlemen." Jayne called over just we were getting started.

"This looks fantastic Jayne. I wonder where the Asian influence comes from. Slow-cooked Moroccan lamb, aromatic roast potatoes, coriander carrots and ...."

"Yes, OK, we like to ring the changes, and yes, we both like Asian food. It's not just my background. It's more to do with all those cooking programs on TV, and the books she keeps buying." I said, tucking into to succulent lamb.

"You keep buying me," Jayne said, "and his mum! Every time we go there she gives me another recipe, but I do like it, and I have learned a lot from her."

We ate. We drank and talked about Michael Parker and Dianne Greenway/Holland. Well, Jonathan and I did. Jayne was more subdued on the subject matter.

"Can we talk about something else for just a while? It's becoming obsessive James," she suddenly came out with, coupled with a look of anxiety I had not seen before.

We fell silent for a while, and I was cross she felt that way at first. Was I involving her for my own ends? I didn't consciously ask her to Ireland thinking she would be as much help as it turned out, but she seemed to be interested in what I was doing as much as I was ... am.

Before I could say anything useful, Jonathan broke the ice. "OK, I can tell you all about my hedonistic holiday in Ibiza this year. I have photos and .."

"OK, OK. I surrender," Jayne shouted, "anything but that ..." she said, almost smiling, and threw her napkin at me.

"Hey, I didn't say anything." I protested.

The atmosphere was back to normal for a while, but both Jonathan and I had taken the hint, and without saying anything dropped the subject of Dianne Greenway, at least until we had finished lunch.

On a Sunday we like to go for a walk to nearby Horsenden Hill, either to work up an appetite, or walk-off a lunch, depending on when we had decided to eat, or just to blow away the cobwebs and enjoy the wonderful views from its high advantage point overlooking London. Today, however, I felt we should press on with Jonathan's analysis of the postcards and see where it takes us next.

With coffee made, we settled back on the sofas and looked at the list again.

Paris, France 12th August 1970. "The question is where she was working between 1970, or earlier, and 1974," I said hoping for suggestions.

"OK," Jonathan replied, "Let's assume she was in Paris. There are some good museums there. So let's mark that WORK. Next."

Cairo, Egypt 23rd October 1974. "Cairo is a must for any archaeologist I would have thought. So, WORK I think. Next."

Rawalpindi, Pakistan 2nd April 1979. "Has to be work," I said. But let's check out the area on Google later."

Seoul, South Korea 21st June 1982. "Again, surely work?"

Delhi, India 6th September 1986. "Again work. But it's a long gap between cards. Don't forget she could have posted these en-route to somewhere else, which makes our task even harder."

Athens, Greece 7th April 1992. "Nice for a holiday, but full of ancient ruins as well. Possibly work and pleasure."

"Do we know what her field of interest was? Most archaeologists specialize in one area; china, art, pottery etc. It may help." Jonathan said, but we did not have that information.

"Good point. I can check back with Leicester Uni to see what she took. Should have thought of that before." I said, cross with myself for missing that. "So let's see how this looks now."

Paris, France 12th August 1970	WORK
Cairo, Egypt 23rd October 1974	WORK
Rawalpindi, Pakistan 2nd April 1979	WORK
Seoul, South Korea 21st June 1982	WORK
Delhi, India 6th September 1986	WORK
Athens, Greece 7th April 1992	WORK or HOLIDAY

We stared at the list blankly. The wine was not helping, so I made some fresh coffee. "No chance of a brandy with that is there?" Jonathan asked hopefully.

"Yes, if we had some. But we forgot the 'duty-free'." I said with a smile. He just frowned.

"What we need to know," Jayne suggested, "is where she was between 1966 and 1970. That may help to piece together how she planned her future. It was the beginning of her career after all if that's what she chose to do, and knowing where she started it would help. Didn't Sinead say something about her returning to London before she came back for Kimberly?"

"Yes, she did. I forgot about that. I wonder if the British Museum knows anything. I still have not had a reply since my visit. Perhaps it's time to call again."

"That sounds like a plan, my boy. Now let me close my eyes and contemplate for a while." At which Jonathan leant back and closed his eyes, looking well-fed and contented.

"Great," I said, "we've got ourselves a squatter."

"I can still hear you," he answered, with eyes closed. "Go and do what you do on a Sunday afternoon, but be quiet about it." And maneuvered to lie horizontally on the sofa.

"Would you like a pillow as well?" I mocked.

"Only if you have one, but don't go and buy one especially," he smirked.

I threw my cushion at him, which he used as a pillow. "Thanks, James."

Jayne looked at me and rested her head on my shoulder as she often does when she can't find the words to say, or just to be close. "Fancy a siesta," I ventured softly.

"Not bloody likely with him in the next room," she whispered back, still with head rested on me. Damn you, friend, I thought, but smiled knowing he would be gone soon.

We did, in fact, have a siesta, on the sofa where we sat. We had nodded off together, and when I awoke, Jayne was still lying on my now numbed shoulder.

I gently lifted her away and laid her down across the length of the sofa. I went to the kitchen to make tea and saw it was nearly five o'clock. Well, I suppose that's what Sundays are for, I tried to convince myself, knowing I still had to find time to check out those city names and write another report for Morris.

I returned to the lounge with mugs of tea just as the phone rang. Jayne, still half asleep, reached over and grabbed the phone. "Mum. Hi. How are you?" Jayne sat up rubbing her eyes with her free hand. She picked up a mug of tea and headed for the bedroom, knowing she could be talking for a while.

The noise had also aroused the other sleeping beauty. "Hell," he exclaimed, "what's the time? Have I missed Match of the Day?" He said sitting upright and blinking away the sleep.

"I have no idea friend. I thought Rugby was your game."

"It is, but I have a wager on Fantasy Football and need an away win at Chelsea today," he said with rather too much concern for my liking.

Just then Jayne reappeared, and he forgot all about football. "That was quick for your mother," I observed. "Only five minutes."

She gave me a look that said be quiet. So I did. "She was in the middle of the Rockies or somewhere, and reception was not very good."

Jonathan and I looked at each other and shrugged. "Well, it wouldn't be, would it, with all those mountains. What's she doing there anyway?" Jonathan asked.

"On holiday covering America and Canada. Twenty cities in fifteen days." Jayne answered. "Rather her than me," she added.

We sipped tea, but I needed a walk. "Anyone fancy a walk? Clear the head . . ."

"I think I should be going," Jonathan said, and stood and stretched. "Things to do, etc. It's been lovely. Thanks, Jayne, great lunch as always." And they kissed goodbye.

"Anytime, Johnny, anytime," she responded.

"I'll work on those cities and contact Leicester tomorrow. Let's catch up on Tuesday lunchtime, and hey, don't forget to speak to your contact about Kimberly Holland." I reminded him.

Jonathan looked at me with a frown. "You called her Holland. Kimberly Holland."

"Well, yes, it just seemed natural I suppose," I said, "Maybe your contact should be looking for Holland and not Greenway."

"I agree. See you Tuesday, but call me first. Bye, Jayne." And I saw him to the door.

"How about that walk," I asked again returning to the lounge.

"How about that siesta," she said with a smile, "then we can walk."

Chapter Eight

Monday morning I was at the boardroom table again going over what I had added to the previous report for Morris when a call came in for me.

"Hello, is that Mr Lacey?" a man's voice asked.

"Yes, speaking."

"Ah, good morning. This is Maurice Fielding from the London Museum." What a coincidence I thought.

"Yes, Mr Fielding how can I help you?"

"I understand you are looking for an employee from around 1966. A Ms Dianne Holland."

My heart was beating a little faster. This was the first time outside of Ireland anyone has referred to her officially as Holland.

"Yes, we have been asked to trace her concerning a possible inheritance," I answered biting my lip.

"Well, she did work here between 1966 to late 1969, having completed her university degree. But where she went from here . . . well, we do not have that information," he said, and my heart sank again.

"Is it possible she worked in Paris, Mr Fielding?" Remembering the postcard list. "Early 1970," but there was a silence. The sort when someone didn't want to say anything rather than thinking for an answer.

"It is possible of course, but as I said . . . we do not know . . ."

"Don't you have a record of supplying any references? If she worked at the British Museum for four years surely she would have given you as a reference . . ."

"That's possible, but I do not see any references here, Mr Lacey. I am sorry I cannot help further."

I couldn't let it go at that. Dangling bait in front of me, and then taking it away. I had to think fast. "If she did go to Paris, where would she have gone, given her specialist area was . . . err . . . I have it here somewhere . . ." Pretending to look through my notes.

"I believe it was ceramics and pottery," he said knowledgeably, "but she could have worked anywhere . . . the Louvre of course, but there are plenty of others for a young archaeologist starting out." He was still being evasive.

I doubt she would have gone straight to the Louvre, but I had to start somewhere.

I wasn't going to get any more from this conversation. "OK, thank you, Mr Fielding . . . one other question . . . did she become well known in her chosen field? Would other archaeologists know her name?" It was a long shot. That silence again.

"Not that I know of, but I am not an archaeologist. Goodbye, Mr Lacey and good luck."

One thing I had not done was search online for her. Just a click of the keypad could answer all my questions. I typed in Dianne Holland, Archaeologist, and pressed "enter".

Nothing appeared of interest. I then tried the same using Greenway. Again nothing. Either she was not prominent in her field and had not published anything or . . . or what? She worked hard and just got on with her job like most people do, without any recognition.

. . .

I printed out my report and knocked on Morris's office door.

"So," he said, still re-reading the sheets of paper, "she could be anywhere in the world. This chap Fielding didn't confirm she went to work in Paris. You are just assuming that from the postcard.

She could have been on holiday," he said in his annoying "summing up" way. If he wanted to be a barrister he should have been one.

"Sir, she didn't go back to Ireland until 1970 when she took her daughter with her. The card after Paris was Cairo 1974. So she could have had a year, maybe two in Paris before applying, or being offered a job in Cairo in '73 or '74. She was studying ceramics and pottery. What better place to expand her career?" I sat staring at Morris. My face felt red but he couldn't know that. I never actually blush, which is a blessing.

Morris stared back, considering what I had just delivered. He saw arguments and counter-arguments in terms of law. He was obviously a frustrated barrister, and I recognized early on this was a line he often likes to take when in meetings.

"Ok," he said slowly, "Mr Parker is anxious to know what we, sorry, you have found so far. I suggest you give him a call, but it's up to you whether you inform him of her real name and the child. Personally, I would not until we know if either is alive. Also, tell him you will check into possible employment in Paris and see where that leads. Is that satisfactory?"

I was almost speechless. When I walked in I was resigned to the fact he would want to tell Parker everything and that was that. Case closed. "Yes, sir. I think that is a good summary of the situation. I will call him now. Thank you." And turned to leave the office, hoping he could not see the delighted expression on my face.

. . .

I called Michael Parker from the boardroom. He sounded excited at the prospect of good news.

Just how would he relish knowing the truth that he had fathered a daughter he has never seen? Did he want to meet her or did he just want to know if she existed? I am sure he has had time to consider these questions, but I also hoped his expectations were not too high.

My call was not overlong. I explained how we had found a link to Ireland via the University, but leaving out the change of name and confirmation of the child. I did confirm we had traced her working in London . . . which was a mistake on reflection. "What! She was working in London after she left Uni. Right under my nose." Silence.

"Are you there, Mr Parker? Are you OK?" Silence.

"Yes." Came the forlorn reply. "What else do have? Anything positive?"

"I could follow up the Paris connection and see if that leads anywhere. After that . . . well, it's up to you how far you want me to go."

"Sorry to sound down James, but my treatment is not going so well. Time is of the essence. Do your best son . . . and by the way . . . go to Paris, don't do it on the phone."

"Are you sure?" I said sounding surprised by the suggestion.

"Yes. Do you speak French?" he asked.

"Some, but a bit rusty in conversational."

"Then take someone with you who can. Speak soon," and he was gone before I could argue further.

Jayne was my first thought, not just because she spoke French, more of her reaction of me going to Paris. What women would wish their partner *bon vacancee* to visit Paris on their own, or with someone who spoke French. I had the rest of the day to get my story right.

"Paris! On your own!" I obviously didn't get my story right. I panicked. "Who said on my own? I didn't say that, did I?" In my best hurt voice.

"Well . . . what are you saying . . . you want me to come with you?" she asked coyly, coming closer now. I made sure I was holding her hands.

"Well, if you can get another couple of days off . . ."

"Yes . . . absolutely. I'll make damn sure I can. When are we going, darling?"

"Hang on . . . I've got a lot of groundwork to do, and I may need your help there. Do you know there are over ninety museums listed in Paris?" I said with some authority.

"Well, I'm not doing ninety museums in two days, my love. There are more interesting places, such as Gallery Lafayette . . ."

"I don't propose to visit ninety museums either, that's why I have a lot of groundwork to do first. I just wish that pompous bloke at the British Museum was more forthcoming. I am sure he knows where she went after London." I said, sounding frustrated.

"Why wouldn't he say, James? If he knew something, there could be something to hide," she said, relishing a scandal.

True, I was sure Fielding was holding back on something, but a scandal! "What more of a scandal could there be than an unmarried mother who abandoned her baby and changed her name," I said rather too abruptly.

"Ah . . . when you put it like that, I see what you mean," she said sourly. "But why would he keep something important back from you if it was going to benefit her," she insisted.

Now, I couldn't argue with that. He had no idea what I knew but didn't what me to know anything about her. "Or he is protecting her from what we already know," I said deep in thought.

"Well deduced, Watson," she said smiling.

"Why am I always Watson, when I have done the deducing?" I complained.

She put her arms around me "You are cute when you frown James," and she kissed me lovingly.

"That's not an answer," I said, kissing her back, "and I don't frown."

Over dinner, we discussed how we could reduce the list of museums to a manageable number. Knowing she was studying ceramics and pottery, we had to identify museums covering those subjects, so we rejected all art museums, fashion, posters, smoking, fans, dental history, sewers, retro, war, textile, science, food, wine, transport, music and many others, on virtually every subject under the sun. After a couple of hours, we had a workable list of just six museums where our Dianne could have studied ceramics and pottery.

Musée du Louvre
Musée National de Céramique-Sèvres
Musée Cernuschi
Musée Cognacq-Jay
Musée National des Arts Asiatiques-Guimet
Musée d'Ennery

"That's a good result, given we started with over ninety," I said, pouring a well-earned glass of wine.

"So what do we do now? Visit them?" Jayne asked.

"Exactly. We have an all-expenses-paid trip, again, and as most of these places are closed on Mondays and Tuesdays, let's go Thursday to Saturday." I said with an air of confidence.

"Oh, wonderful. I've never been on Eurostar. Do you want to go this week?"

"Can you get time off at short notice?"

"For Paris? Of course, I can," she said, looking very happy.

. . .

I booked the 8.02am from St. Pancras for Thursday, and made a list of the addresses we needed to visit. In my eagerness, I nearly forgot to book a hotel. I eventually found something central. Not too expensive, but also not too cheap. It pays to spend a little more in Paris for a good room.

We arrived at the Hotel Paris et Choiseul around 11.30am and quickly located the first museum to visit. Musée National de Céramique-Sèvres.

It was a short Metro ride just south of the Seine, then a five-minute walk. The building was impressive. Every inch a museum built in the neo-classical style with east and west wings and a wide sweeping stone staircase entrance. Inside, however, as with large established museums, it had an air of the 21st century about it. Like the British Museum, it had been transported from the darkness of the eighteenth century to the age of light and openness. We found the information desk and I put Jayne to work.

"Est il possible de parler à quelqu'un dans le recrutement ou au personnel svp?"

"Pourquoi donc?" the woman asked sourly.

"We are trying to trace someone who may have worked here in 1970. We are from a London solicitors firm and need to find this lady." Jayne handed my business card to the woman and turned to me looking defeated already. "This is going to take forever James. Are two days going to be enough?"

"Have some faith my love. You are doing great. I reckoned we can do two more today and easily the other three tomorrow. If we strike lucky before then, fantastic." I said with a smile. "We will have more time for sightseeing – but not museums."

"Agreed," she smiled back. The woman behind the desk put down the phone and told us to wait while someone came to see us.

"This is the same procedure I went through in London. They will probably take the details and call us later," and within two minutes a tall, smart, attractive looking lady approached us, well me, and spoke in perfect English. "I understand you wanted to see me. I am Marie Renoir head of recruitment."

After the introductions, I explained our visit and gave her a sheet of paper detailing what we wanted to know; names, dates etc., in both English and French. She looked at the paper. "You are very thorough, Mr Lacey." I tried to hide my modesty but Jayne decided to have the last word. "Yes, well he is a solicitor. Please call us on that number if you can. Thank you for your time, Madam." And Jayne ushered me out of the building.

"Hey, what's the rush?" I complained.

"We have to find the other places."

"Come on . . . Jayne . . . you didn't like me talking to her . . ."

"Let's just say it's a good job I came."

We located the next museum and sat quietly on the Metro. I never thought of Jayne being the jealous type. Was it just Paris? Does it have that effect on people? She has never shown any sign of jealousy back in London when we have been out together. And I have never had reason to be jealous of her. She is friendly, but never flirty with guys, although there is the exception that is Jonathan, whom she winds-up more than flirts with.

I decided not to pursue the point further.

The next port of call was Musée Cernuschi, back in the center of Paris next to the Parc de Monceau. This museum was smaller but still very impressive. Its collections spanned three floors of mainly Chinese and South Asian art, ceramics and statues. We presented ourselves at the information desk.

This time there was no one to see us, so we left the printout and asked for someone to contact us as soon as possible.

Back outside the June sun was very warm. The sky was blue and we were in Paris. "Come on," I said, "let's treat ourselves to lunch," and we walked through the adjacent park de Monceau into the Rue de Phalsbourg, and found a suitable pavement restaurant. The restaurant, although suitable, was not the main reason for lunch. Anyone who has been to Paris knows the delights of pavement eating on a warm day. "It's not the best I've seen, but I'll find a really good one tonight, and we will have a romantic dinner for two under the Paris stars."

"Don't go spending your client's money on expensive meals. He may not appreciate it if we don't get any results." Jayne said, enjoying her herb omelet and fries.

"OK, I promise it won't be too expensive. Now, where do we go from here?" I asked, laying out the street map on the table.

The next one was Musée Cognacq-Jay. "But as the crow flies the Musée Guimet is only a short walk from here."

"OK, let's walk off lunch," she agreed, and we set off in what I hoped was the right direction.

"I was reading about this place on the train coming over. It has one of the largest and most beautiful collections of ceramics and sculptures from all over Asia."

"Yes, but so does the Louvre," she suggested.

"True, but I have this gut feeling she wouldn't have gone to the Louvre. Don't forget she was here for only one to two years. I just don't feel the Louvre would have been right for her."

The Guimet is again an old building, but with newly added courtyards and entrance to give the visitor a modern 21st-century approach. Inside you are greeted with a magnificent spectacle of color and subtle light. Of the museums we have seen, I felt I could spend more time in here, discovering its many treasures across the four floors from India, Japan, China and the Asian peninsula. Jayne talked the talk, and soon we were approached by a very well dressed elderly gentleman.

"Qui, I am Louis de la Lodge. I understand you are looking for an employee from 1970."

"Yes, we are trying to see if she is in line for an inheritance," I said.

Monsieur de la Lodge looked at each of us in turn and shrugged. "I don't know if we have records that far back. The whole department was moved in 1986 and not everything is on computer. And even if we did have her on record, I am not sure we could give out personal details," he stated, almost too perfectly, looking at the document I handed him.

"I have been here for forty years and do not recognize this name. I am sorry I cannot be of help." And he turned to leave us standing there, empty.

"What about the name Greenway, Monsieur," I called out. More in desperation. He stopped and turned. "I thought you said Holland was the name, which is it?" He was starting to get impatient. "Greenway was her birth name," I said, but still no response and he turned again to leave.

"The daughter would have been around five years old. Kimberly was her name." Jayne called out.

He paused long enough to tell me he recognized the name. Anyone else would have carried on walking.

"Please Monsieur," Jayne stepped forward. She hadn't said anything since speaking French to the receptionist. "We only want to know if she or her daughter is still alive. Nothing more."

Slowly he turned. Shoulders slightly hunched. "Come with me."

We followed him up a flight of stairs and through a door marked privé. Now we were back in what we know museums to look like behind the walls. Narrow, dark passages with other passages leading off left and right. A labyrinth. All museums have them, and the older they are the more passages they have.

We eventually came into a well-lit room - our eyes having to adjust to the light again. "Please sit down," and he gestured to two rather old upright chairs opposite his desk.

He looked at us and removed his glasses. "Yes, I knew Dianne Holland."

I looked at Jayne and reached out for her hand.

"I started here in 1966 straight from the Sorbonne. The museum was full of objects to be catalogued and they took in dozens of students or graduates over the summer recess. Dianne joined us in, I think it was 1969 or late 1970, and was here for two years." He looked down, as people do when remembering. He smiled. "We became lovers. She moved in with me, and life was wonderful."

We said nothing. I didn't want to interrupt the flow of memories he had not spoken to anyone about for so long, but had probably thought them every day.

"London was the capital of pop and fashion back then, but Paris was the center for art and jazz, and, like London, we were re-discovering our National treasures denied to us for so long during the war, as well as the new jazz scene from America.

They all came; Coltrane, Monk, Davis . . ," he stopped mid-sentence, "sorry, this is not of interest."

"Yes, it is," I said quickly, not wanting him to lose his thoughts.

"It's fascinating, really." Jayne nodded her confirmation.

"You are very kind. An old man's memories are . . . well, just that, memories. No one, especially young people want to know about the old days. I suppose it's the same all over the world now." And he paused again, deep in personal thought.

"Monsieur, did Dianne go to Cairo after Paris?" I asked tentatively, hoping to bring him around to later events.

He gave me a puzzled look. "How did you know that?"

"We have a list of countries we think she worked in," Jayne answered. "She sent her sister a postcard from Cairo in 1972."

"Yes, it is true. She wanted to do more fieldwork and was starting to focus more on Islamic culture and ceramics. She said she felt stifled here after two years, so when she was offered a post in Cairo I was . . . heartbroken."

He stood up and walked over to a shelf and returned with a black & white photo. "This is us on the fountain at Tuileries six months before she left."

Jayne took it and smiled. "You both look very happy," she said passing it to me.

This was the first image I had ever seen of Dianne Holland, albeit forty years old. I at least now had an image of her in my mind. I handed it back to him without comment.

"Monsieur, we are here until Saturday. Could we have dinner with you tonight, and perhaps hear more of your story?" It was a long shot, but I sensed he would talk less emotionally away from the museum.

Jayne nodded. "Yes, that would be a good idea, please say yes Monsieur."

Monsieur Louis de la Lodge smiled gently. "Mademoiselle, I can never refuse a lady's invitation to dinner . . . but on one condition."

We looked at each other, expecting a stipulation in the conversation . . . "I choose the restaurant and I pay," he said, smiling and standing.

We exchanged telephone numbers and gave him our address. He was to collect us at 7.45pm outside our hotel.

We took a taxi back to our hotel. "What a lovely old man," Jayne said leaning back on the black leather taxi seats. "He really wants to talk about her doesn't he James."

I was only half-listening to her. I was watching the traffic and the multi-colored Paris landscape in front of me constantly changing shape like a kaleidoscope. "James . . . what are you thinking?"

"Sorry love, not sure really. The last time we quizzed an elderly person about Dianne Holland, they died the same day."

Jayne looked at me in horror. "Don't say that, James. That's awful." And slapped me, not too hard, on the shoulder.

I reassured her with a smile and touched her cheek. "He liked you. Obviously still a 'ladies' man'."

Back in the hotel room, I called Jonathan with the news. Why not Morris first? He was delighted but still had no news for me on the Kimberly search. I did call Morris but he was in a meeting. I thought of phoning Michael Parker but decided against it until, at least, we had had dinner with the enigmatic Louis de la Lodge.

. . .

The taxi arrived at 7.45pm sharp and we joined M. de la Lodge for the short ride across central Paris, past the Opera and along Boulevard des Italians turning right into the long, narrow and busy Boulevard Haussmann. The taxi dropped us on the corner of Passage Jouffroy, next to the Wax Works Museum. The Jouffroy is one of several 'passages' that are long and narrow, where almost every establishment is a restaurant, café or bar. The area was busy and we had trouble keeping sight of Louis as he led us further into this Parisian labyrinth. Suddenly he held aloft his ebony and ivory cane to indicate we had arrived, and we found ourselves entering the wonderful restaurant which was L'Etoile.

"I hope you have booked Monsieur." I said whispered. The restaurant was full already and only just 8.00pm.

Louis half-turned and smiled. "Of course. Follow me." And without waiting for a waiter to seat us, he moved forward between the aisle of diners, to what I saw was an empty round table at the right-hand corner of this bustling restaurant. As soon as we approached the table two waiters dressed in traditional black and white were ready to seat us.

"You did book. I think you have been here before." I whispered across the table.

He smiled and nodded. "Just a few times."

A moment later the maître d' came and shook hands with Louis. We were introduced in turn, but instead of shaking our hand, he nodded in response to our names. "Do you like wine . . . silly question I know, but these days one has to ask?"

"We do, Monsieur." Jayne confirmed.

"Bon, but one rule I have, please, you call me Louis."

"Thank you," Jayne said, "and we are Jayne and James."

"OK, formalities out of the way, will you allow me to order the wine?"

"Of course," I said, "If it doesn't have Sainsbury's on it I'm lost anyway," and laughed too loudly. Jayne closed her eyes and shook her head. Louis looked at me with a glazed expression.

"Sorry, Louis. Just James's attempt at humor," she said in my defense.

Looking around at our fellow diners I noticed how smart most were. Why do the French look good even when in casuals? French women however always seem to look elegant without effort. Maybe that's the secret – not to worry too much. Be natural.

Not that Jayne looked out of place. In fact, she has the ability to dress amazingly, whatever the occasion.

The restaurant was long and narrow, with a row of tables each side of the aisle, each seating four people.

I realized then we had the only round table in the room. Behind us were a pair of ornate wooden doors with elegantly engraved glass etchings, on frosted panels. Louis informed us that behind the doors was a private dining room.

"I hope you approve of the restaurant. I can recommend everything." Louis said with a warm smile.

"It's wonderful, it's so. . . French." Jayne said raising her glass. "To a very pleasant evening," and we toasted our host and sipped the wine.

"So," I said, wanting to learn more of Dianne Holland. That was of course why we were here. "When did you first know of the child . . ." Louis raised his hand, his forefinger pointing at me, swaying from side to side. "No, James. I have a rule. We do not talk business until at least dessert. Agreed?"

I shrugged, the way the French do. "No problem," was all I could say without looking too disappointed.

The next half hour was spent discussing the menu. Between Jayne translating, and Louis describing each and every Entrée, I could see this meal going on for some time.

We eventually ordered, and after a couple of glasses of wine, I felt a little more relaxed.

"How long have you been coming here, Louis?" I asked with interest.

He smiled thoughtfully. "Let me see . . . it was 1983. You see, I never married. My work became my wife and my mistress. I lived alone with two cats, but sadly no more," he frowned. "I was made head of my department in 1981 with a good salary, so I decided it was better to eat out well than eat alone sadly."

"So you come here a lot?" Jayne asked.

"I found it by accident," he continued, "but like many precious and wonderful things, many are found like that, especially in my world of antiquities."

We nodded in quiet agreement. "After ten years of patronage, they gave me my own table, here. Always available no matter how full the restaurant is," he said gesturing to the full room with a certain amount of justified pride.

"How lovely." Jayne said, with genuine respect.

The starters of warm Fois Gras, and the main of roasted Pigeon were followed by cheese. Did this constitute a dessert?

"So, Louis . . . you and Dianne . . ."

"Non," he was almost smiling, and I suspect he was enjoying this. "James, this is cheese, not dessert. Is that so, Jayne?"

"Hey, I don't want to be outnumbered, Louis. OK, I surrender. No more talk," and raised my hands yet again.

He promptly changed the subject "So what of you two? Are you married?"

"No," Jayne answered coyly, looking straight at me.

"And James, where are you from?"

My stock answer. "Acton, West London. . ."

"No, not where you live, I mean your family's home. India I would guess."

That's the second time I've been asked that recently. "My Grandparents left India in 1946 during the Partition.

Their family settled in southern India, Kerala."

I noticed then the chatter from around me had subsided, and I could hear my own voice without having to raise it. Looking around, in fact, there were only two other people left in the restaurant. It was 11.30pm. "Wow. I hadn't realized it was so late." I said looking at Jayne, but she wasn't worried at all. She was radiant and enjoying the evening. We sipped brandy and drank coffee, and talked about ourselves. Our work, our flat, our likes and dislikes . . . in fact, everything except Dianne Holland.

"My friends, it is midnight and an old man like me needs his sleep. Not that I work much now at my age, but they let me go in a couple of days a week, and tomorrow being Friday I have some paperwork to finalize," he suddenly announced.

"But, sir . . . Louis, we haven't yet talked . . ." And again, he raised his hand, shaking it slowly. "Forgive me, James," He said looking at Jayne, and then at me with a tired smile. He reached down and placed on the table a small translucent blue paper bag with twisted handles, held together by a matching blue velvet bow. He set it in front of Jayne. She looked at me for help but I had no idea what he was doing. "One month before she left, I brought her this Christmas present." Jayne touched her lips, but it was her eyes that were glazing over. "She left on December 23rd, a week earlier than planned. I never got the chance to give it to her. It has been in my apartment ever since, wrapped, as I bought it." His hand was shaking slightly as he pushed the blue package across the table towards Jayne.

Instinctively she took his hand to steady it, and the shaking eased. Jayne shook her head in anticipation of what he was proposing. "I can't Louis, I can't," she said, now with tears running down her cheek.

Louis de la Lodge smiled and nodded. "Oui. I would be honored if you would take this memory from me, my dear." And he stood up, releasing her hand before kissing it. "James. I have not deceived you. I love company and good food, and I have had both this evening." He reached into his inside jacket pocket and gave me a sealed envelope. "I have written here, in

English, all I think you need to know about Dianne Holland." And he handed me the envelope, but before letting go added,

"There is one more rule. Please do not contact me again after tonight. Do you understand?" He said with a seriousness in his tone I had not heard from him before but knew full well what he meant. I nodded. He released the envelope and smiled again.

We said goodbye outside the restaurant and noticed we were the last to leave, and from the expression on the garcons face's, not a moment too soon.

Jayne and Louis kissed cheek to cheek, and we shook hands. "Thank you for dinner, and everything," I said warmly, taking hold of Jayne's free hand. We walked the now relatively empty passage back to Boulevard

Haussmann where he hailed a taxi, but he did not offer to travel with us. Then he was gone, leaving us bewildered and bemused, to find our own way back to the hotel.

Jayne, for the second time that day, laid her head on my shoulder and closed her eyes, albeit for fifteen minutes. Part of me felt cheated. Louis de la Lodge knew we wanted to hear about Dianne's work and life in Paris, but he strung us along, knowing all the while he was holding all the cards. The gift to Jayne. The letter I was holding. All planned. The other part of me, however, was dying to read his account of their life in 1970's Paris.

"Hey," I said gently touching her shoulder, "let's see what this forty-year-old gift is."

Jayne sat up and lifted the carrier bag onto the seat between us, and nervously pulled on the blue velvet bow. She lifted out the wrapped box and started to gently peel away the tissue paper.

"It's heavy, whatever it is," Jayne said completing the task to reveal a plain cardboard box. She pulled at the sticky tape with a fingernail and opened the top. The suspense was getting to me, and we were nearly back at the hotel. "Come on. We're nearly home." I said rather impatiently.

"James, this is delicate. We are unwrapping the past here. Forty years of memories. We must be considerate."

I smiled and touch her hand. "Sorry, you are right as usual."

She pulled back the tissue paper to reveal the top of a white pearl box. She lifted it out, and we stared at the most stunning mother of pearl box. It was around six inches square with a gilt hinged lid.

We looked at each other. "Any guesses?" she said opening the lid. From the odor, we could only conclude it was, in fact, a tea caddy. "Of course. Don't you remember Sinead saying she loved tea, and I bet she didn't use teabags back then."

"It's lovely, but not practical now. I suppose I could use it as a jewelry box," and gave me a knowing smile, which I ignored.

"If Louis bought it as an antique back then, I wonder what it's worth today." But before we could consider any sudden rise in our financial circumstances, we had arrived at our hotel.

Then there was the envelope he had given me, but I realized by the time we reached our bedroom that neither of us was capable of reading, let alone understanding and analyzing the content of Louis's letter.

We somehow crawled into bed feeling content. We had been dined and wined and been thoroughly entertained. I put aside my earlier contempt and drifted into a sweet sleep with the knowledge I had all of tomorrow to play detective, again.

Over breakfast, my expectations of reading a full and frank account of their lives together turned to disappointment, and then frustration. "Damn," I said out loud, but no one seemed to take notice except Jayne.

"James, not so loud. What is it?"

"Nothing! That's the point. Nothing we don't already know. Just two pages of typed . . . reminiscences I suppose . . ." I put down the typed sheets, and Jayne snatched them up.

"I see what you mean," she said without looking up, "he's reliving the time they had together," she looked at me with a sad expression. "I think we gave him absolution in a way. He wanted to write it all down . . . almost like . . ." she searched for a word, "exorcising the past."

"Oh, hell Jayne, that sounds kind of final, doesn't it?" I said staring back at her. "You don't think he's going to do anything . . . silly."

She took a sharp intake of breath. "James, don't joke . . . I couldn't handle another death." Which unfortunately was overheard by one or two of our fellow dinners. "Come on. We need to make a call."

"I haven't finished my croissant," she complained as I guided her out of the dining room and into the street. Louis de la Lodge had used museum paper to type his confessional which had the address and telephone number on. I dialed the number. "Bonjour. Musée Guimet." I passed the phone to Jayne. "Quick, do your French thing. Ask for him. He said he would be in today." I said quickly.

"What am I supposed to say?"

"Anything . . . just ask for him before she hangs up."

"Oui, bonjour . . . M.de la Lodge s'il vous plait." Jayne said looking daggers at me.

Silence . . . . "He's not there," I said in a panic and started pacing up and down in front of the hotel.

"Oui . . . good morning Louis, yes, it's Jayne here . . . we just wanted to say thank you again for a lovely evening . . . yes, it was a lovely meal. Anyway, we just wanted to let you know how much we enjoyed it . . . yes, we will . . . goodbye, Louis . . . yes, I will."

She closed the phone and handed it back to me. "See, he's there," she said with an air finality. "Can we go shopping now?"

Louis de la Lodge replaced the receiver and allowed himself a half-smile. *"Please find her mes amis"* he whispered, blinking away a tear.

Chapter Nine

Paris had been worth a visit if only to have met Louis. I could justify that, but had we actually learnt anything? Well, yes I suppose so. Louis had confirmed she worked in Paris, and she travelled to Cairo with her daughter, Kimberly, in 1970.

It was Sunday again, and somehow Jonathan had invited himself around for lunch. "So, where's my pressie from gay Pari . . . ?

"One, it was not a holiday, and second . . . if anyone deserves a present it would be Jayne." I said, knowing she could hear me from the kitchen.

"Thank you, my love. I will remember that on our next trip," she called back.

"Next trip!" I went into the kitchen to confront her, and Jonathan followed, hoping for a 'domestic'."

"What next trip?" I asked with genuine concern.

"She's right of course, James," he said, picking at the naan bread, "now we have a first-hand account of the start of her career, we are on the way to finding out more, but I think we need to look closely at the choices we have and be very mindful of the places she sent the remaining cards from." He picked up the postcards and laid them out again on the dining table in date order.

Jayne stopped stirring the curry, and we all looked at the row of postcards again, for the hundredth time.

"What are you looking at now, James?" Jayne asked, but before I could give my opinion, Jonathan shot in.

"Well my fellow sleuths, let's assume ALL these places are work-related, therefore it would be practical to start at the last place we have, which is Athens, and work backwards."

"I see," I said blankly, "but there is still the question of knowing where she was working. At least we know she went to Cairo - Louis confirms that, so that saves us time not having to visit a dozen or so places she could have been at."

Jonathan realized the flaw in his hypothesis. "Damn, you are right of course. Each of the other places of work should, in theory, be able to provide where she went next."

"Are you saying we have to visit ALL of these places, in turn, to find out where her next job was?" Jayne asked, somewhat frustratedly.

"Well . . . no . . . not all, probably . . ." I said, trying not to commit to anything whilst she was holding a wooden spoon. "Hey, the curry must be done by now, I for one am starving."

"James Lacey," she said waving the wooden spoon in my face, "we will talk about this over lunch. Now clear those off the table please and pour me a glass of wine. I think I'm going to need it."

We ate in silence for a while, well, at least not taking about Dianne, but I was thinking what our next step should be when I suddenly realized I used "our" and not "my". What started out for me as a misguided quest by a dying old man has suddenly turned into . . . a what . . . I looked at Jayne and Jonathan and smiled.

"Bloody hellfire," Jonathan exclaimed. "What have you put in his curry, Jayne?"

"I'm fine," I confirmed, "the curry is fine. We are all fine, aren't we?"

Jayne stopped eating. "James, don't scare me, what is it?"

"I was just thinking out loud, that's all. What started as a simple job which should have taken a few days, has turned into a very interesting pursuit of the truth thanks to you two."

"Group hug," Jonathan said, ready to stand.

"Sit!" Jayne ordered, and he leant back with his usual forlorn look, which doesn't work on either of us.

"What I mean is, this is becoming far more interesting than I ever imagined. I *really* want to know if Dianne Greenway is dead or alive. Where is Kimberly? . . that's a point, has your contact come up with anything on her Johnny?"

He ignored the Johnny. "No," he said looking apologetic. "Nothing found in Ireland or the UK under any combination of Kimberly Holland or Kimberly Greenway. And yes, we have tried all the different spellings of the name Kimberly with no luck. Now that can mean one of two possibilities." He took a sip of wine. "One, she is not registered in the UK or Ireland, or she has married."

"Oh, hell." I said in frustration, "I had not thought of that . . . married. But that could have been anywhere."

"Yes," Jayne said, "married anywhere, and living anywhere. Now that is a needle in a haystack."

"OK then, we concentrate on the mother, agreed?" I suggested, and put forward my next idea very carefully.

"Let's see what places we can find in Rawlpindi, Seoul and Delhi on the net, and see what can be found by calling them first."

"First!" Jayne spotted my error.

"Well . . . I mean it's a starting point . . . if we . . I . . . have to ask old man Parker for permission to go further afield, then that's a real possibility." I was glad she was sitting opposite me, but my ankles were still at risk.

I gave Rawalpindi to Jonathan, Seoul to Jayne and I took Delhi.

"We only have one laptop," Jayne stated the obvious.

"OK, we take turns." I was going to suggest, but she had another idea."

"How about we leave it alone today and go for a long walk. It's a glorious July Sunday and you want to work!"

Jonathan and I looked at each other and realized we had no defense. So we walked, and I was glad we did. It was a beautiful day, but, like the other two, I suspect, we were already listing out the possibilities in our head of the outcome of our research, and the inevitable scenario that I would have to plan for a longer trip, to another continent.

. . .

Monday found me in the boardroom again preparing my report when the mobile rang. It was Michael Parker. "James, sorry to be a bore, but just wanted to know how Paris went."

I cursed under my breath. I wanted to prepare something first, not give an off-the-cuff answer, but it seems I will have to. "Hello, sir. It went well actually. We did meet someone who worked with Dianne and he remembers her well."

"That sounds good James. What did he tell you about her? Is she alive?"

"Mr Parker, this gentleman knew her a long time ago. They were colleagues. He remembers she left to go to Cairo, but that is all we have."

"Excellent. Cairo of course. Lots of archaeology interest there. When are you going, James?"

The tone of his voice was one of elation. He thinks I am going to find her and bring her home to him. "I can do some research and make some calls without actually going to Cairo. Let me do that and let's see what I have in a few days, and then you can make a decision."

"OK, James, I understand," his tone now was not so jubilant, "but call me soon. I feel we are getting close."

The office was quiet for a Monday. Raj was on holiday and Morris was in court with a client. Only Mr Wicks was in our department. "Morning, sir."

"James, stop calling me sir. Makes me sound much older than I care to be."

"Sorry. Just habit I suppose."

"Come and sit down and tell me what you are up to with Mr Parker." I didn't know how much Mr Wicks knew or wanted to know. He was probably just being polite.

"Well," I said, sitting opposite him at his desk, "not sure how much you know, but Mr Parker called me in around four weeks ago and wanted me to find a long lost girlfriend."

Wicks showed no surprise on hearing this and allowed me to continue.

"We . . . I . . . that is, did not have much to go on, but I did have some help from a friend at Frasier and Frasier, and we eventually traced her to Ireland, then Paris and now it seems Cairo."

Wicks sat nodding with interest. "What was this lady's name," he asked eventually.

"Dianne Greenway . . . well no actually, he knew her as Dianne Holland."

Wicks leant forward and stared at me as if in a trance.

"Say that name again, James."

"Dianne Holland . . . or Greenway . . . she seems to have changed her name after leaving Ireland," but Wicks had looked away from me, and was staring into space.

"Dianne . . . Holland . . . that name is familiar to me James. It can't just be coincidence, can it," he said, and his face reddened, and I thought he was going to have a heart attack.

"Are you OK, sir? Can I get you some water?"

"Yes please, James," he whispered, leaning back in his chair and closing his eyes.

I grabbed a bottle of water from the fridge and ran back to the office. "Damn, sorry, forgot the glass."

"No matter, James," and he sipped the water, which was when I noticed his hand was shaking.

"Dianne Holland, was that it? What does that name mean to you?" I asked, as sympathetically as possible. But before he could answer Mr Morris came in not looking too pleased.

"Hello, Charles, can I have a word," he asked in his usual manner.

I took my leave, nodding to Morris as I left. "Oh, James, do see me later with an update," he added as I reached the office door.

"Yes, sir, of course," and I left them to it.

What had got Wicks all hot and bothered? Was it coincidence, or did he recognize the name? That would have to wait, I had to type my Paris report and catch up on what Raj had left me. Trust him to go on holiday now.

I called Jonathan at around 2.00 o'clock. "Hi, any luck with Rawalpindi?"

"Hello to you too. You sound down."

"Sorry, just a bad workday. So what news?"

"Well, I have not been idle. I found one museum in Rawalpindi, but I don't think it would have suited our lady. Not her field of interest, but I will email you the details and you can take it from there."

"Well, it's a start. Thanks, Johnny. I'll keep you posted on what Jayne and I find out tonight."

I wasn't sure if Jayne had had time at work to do any private investigating, but my mind kept wandering back to Charles Wicks. I opened the laptop and Googled Charles Wicks, Solicitor.

Very few hits appeared, in fact just two; one dead, one in a law firm in Perth. Then I saw our website, Morris, Sterne and Wicks providing Family mediation,

Conveyancing, Wills & Probate and all Business & Commercial matters. The rest of the website blurb went on to describe each division and who headed it. It still had Mr Sterne as head of Wills & Probate, so I guess they have not agreed on a new partner yet.

Under the Partner Profile, I read Charles Wicks's entry.

Admitted as a solicitor in 1971 and practiced in the area of Weybridge until his move to London in 1990. He joined Morris & Sterne in partnership in 1992. Charles undertakes all types of work for his clients and is experienced in many areas of Law. Currently, Charles is semi-retired and works three days a week, and is our expert in the complex area of Landlord and Tenant and Commercial Law.

Except he is working five days a week covering for the late Mr Sterne. The web page photographs of each of the partners were professionally taken, although they had not been updated for a good few years. Mr Wicks looks about thirty. His clients must have a shock when they finally meet him. I wasn't sure what I wanted, or expected to find on Charles Wicks, but my nagging doubts followed me for the rest of the day.

Chapter Ten

I got home that evening around 7.00pm and Jayne was still not back. I opened some pasta and boiled the kettle then checked my emails. Mostly spam, but Jonathan had sent details of the museum he found in Rawalpindi, the Taxila Museum. I checked out their website. He was right. Probably not of interest to our Dianne, but I did notice it was a base for a local "dig" that started in 1917 and is still ongoing. I remembered Louis saying something about her wanting to do more fieldwork or digs. If Cairo was interesting then it is plausible she wanted to look for work further afield. I found the email address and composed a letter.

Dear Sirs

I am writing on behalf of a client trying to find the whereabouts of a possible former employee, She would have worked for the museum between 1976 - 1984.

Her name is Dianne Holland and her specialist area was in ancient ceramics.

I would appreciate any information you may have as we are eager to contact Ms Holland in the matter of an inheritance.

Yours sincerely
James Lacey
Morris, Sterne & Wicks Solicitors, London

Well, it's a long shot I told myself, but probably better than a phone call. But if not Taxila, then where? I needed a map of Pakistan. I found my Phillips World Atlas, published 1991.

That needed updating, thinking of all the changes that have happened to countries since this was published.

Significantly the split of Yugoslavia and Czechoslovakia in Europe and the break-up of the Soviet Union where many countries that were unknown to me have suddenly been reborn, and the world map is crammed with more countries than you would think possible to print on one page. I turned my attention to Asia and in particular Pakistan. Rawalpindi is situated in the North of the country, and I wanted to make a note of other nearby large cities that may have museums worthy of Ms. Holland's attention.

Islamabad, however, was the only noteworthy contender, being just thirty miles to the north, and the capital of Pakistan.

I leant back and rubbed my eyes. There are too many variables here. She could have sent the postcard on a visit to Rawalpindi, and be staying, well, almost anywhere. I needed food. Jayne was still not home and had not texted me. I called her mobile but no answer, and then I remembered something about a leaving drink with some colleagues. So pasta for one.

"Hey, sleepy-head," Jayne said, gently touching my arm. I had fallen asleep on the sofa with the laptop open.

"Hey, you're back. How was it?" I said, moving the laptop onto the floor.

"OK, actually. Went to a nice pub in Slough and had some bar food. So, what have you been up to, apart from sleeping?"

"I got my own supper, and washed up from this morning," I said rather grumpily.

Jayne was next to me now, and she put her arms around me and cuddled up close. "Sorry," she said demurely, "I was only kidding," and kissed my cheek.

We sat a while just cuddling. It does give me a warm and secure feeling. I am sure an analyst would say I have a mother complex by feeling safe in a woman's arms. Jayne could see I was thinking out loud. She always can. "Want to share?" she asked.

"Share what?"

"James Lacey, I may have only known you for a short time, but I know when something is troubling you," she said smugly.

We disentwined. "Well, I had been going over the Pakistan possibilities, but it's not just that." I retrieved my laptop. "It's the whole thing. I don't know if it's even possible to find her. Why not tell Parker we have tried and we have gone as far as we can with no concrete answer either way." I was almost cuddling the laptop.

Jayne leant back on the sofa and gave me one of her summing-up looks. "So, after all your/our, hard work, you want to throw in the towel. OK, I agree." I was taken by surprise, and it showed. "Well," she continued, "you did ask."

"Yes, but I didn't expect you to agree so readily," I said, now sounding defensive.

"Look," she said, taking my hand, "you need to weigh up the pros and cons. Is what you have achieved so far more than expected, and what are the chances of obtaining more information that will lead you to even more positive results?"

"Wow, I forgot you took psychology," I said smiling.

"Only for one year, but it helped with my business studies. So what do we have and what do we need," she continued, standing up and stretching.

"Sleep, I think. Let's look at it in the morning." So we went to bed and forgot, almost, all about Dianne Holland.

. . .

Mr Majid Patel, the curator of the Taxila Museum, studied the email again. In 1976 Majid was only ten years old, and had no ambition to study history or archaeology, or anything remotely to do with museums. Majid Patel was going to be a famous cricketer, along with every other ten-year-old in the country, but he was even more determined to achieve that goal, being named after one of Pakistani's most famous batsmen, Majid Khan. Majid even made history on the young Majid's birthday in 1976 by becoming one of the few batsmen to score a century in seventy-four balls. The omens were all there. He just needed to be spotted by the cricket scouts at his school, and his future would be secured.

Majid touched his left leg and scratched his knee, just under the where the caliper rests. "Damn itching," he said out loud and closed the computer screen he had been staring at. He was feeling too tired now to make any enquiries, and besides, it will mean going down into the archive rooms, which he does not intend to do on account of his leg. Majid's hopes of imitating his hero were shattered six months after his tenth birthday when he was diagnosed with polio. He had seen the effects of it in his village but never thought it would happen to him. He was the chosen one. The omens were there . . . why did it all go wrong? He asked himself these questions for many years, but he could never come to terms with his condition.

. . .

Over breakfast, Jayne continued her amateur analyzing techniques on me. "So, my lovely, tell me again why you want to give up on Dianne Holland."

"It's not that I want to," I said, still half asleep, "it's more not having, or ever being in possession of some concrete evidence that she is alive."

Jayne sat there staring at me, expecting me to continue, or so it seemed.

"James, every great detective has a moment of foreboding until that final clue is unearthed. Do you think Einstein gave up on his first attempt to discover the meaning of relativity! Did Darwin give up because he was hounded by religious fundamentalists! . . ."

"Hey, slow down love, I get the message," I said, walking over to her and hugging her.

"Sorry," she muttered into my dressing gown. "I was just trying to show you that you don't have to give up at the first obstacle. We can do this, all three of us . . ."

I stepped back a-ways but was still holding her hands. I looked her up and down, twice.

"Hey, silly, you me and Jonathan - who did you think I meant?"

. . .

In the office, Morris had left a message saying Mr Parker had called and wanted to meet with me. I really did not want a face-to-face meeting just now - I could not see the point of it, except to say, sorry, I have done as much as possible, and your Dianne Holland is not to be found, dead or alive.

I checked my emails hoping for some good news, but just the opposite. Nothing back from Pakistan, but an email from the Garda in Cork, requesting the presence of James Lacey and Jayne Wood to attend the coroner's inquest on the death of Sinead Greenway, on the 1st August. That's all I needed, and it's only 11 o'clock. Maybe Jonathan can cheer me up.

"Hi, Johnny, what news?"

"None, if you keep calling me Johnny."

"Sorry, just wanted to hear some good news. Jayne had a go at me this morning for wanting to give up, and now we have to go back to Cork for the sister's inquest next week."

"Well, I have nothing more than I gave you on that museum. Did you write to them?"

"Yes, but I have not heard back. Maybe I will call them in case the email went astray. I just need another lead. We seem to have hit a brick wall."

"What about Cairo? Did you call them yet? They may still have some idea where she went in Pakistan."

"Yes, I will. Thanks for reminding me, Jonathan. Let's have lunch tomorrow and catch up."

"Now you're talking. Usual place one o'clock. Love to Jayne."

I needed to focus if I was to get through this period of self-doubt, so I checked time-lines in Cairo and Rawalpindi. Egypt is two hours ahead, and Pakistan is plus six hours.

One problem was that Louis did not say which museum she went to in Cairo. On checking Wikipedia I found over twenty-five museums alone in Cairo, including the largest, The Egyptian Museum of Antiquities. I leant back in my chair and stared at the ceiling hoping to see a sign. My mother says we are driven by fate, not luck. I have never believed in either - maybe - until now. The office curtains were drawn to provide some shade from the bright sunlight. These curtains were not lined, so the delicately printed pattern was casting a shadow on the ceiling at that moment I glanced upwards. I was looking at what could only be described as a mosaic, albeit quite abstract, but the look and feel of the design was unmistakable.

Louis had said Dianne left because she was offered a job related to Islamic ceramics. It certainly narrowed the odds, and I studied the list of museums in Cairo with renewed interest.

. . .

Majid Patel felt the pain in his left leg on each step of the old stairwell leading down to the archive rooms. The museum had only installed computers in 1997 but did not have the resources or funds to upload all of the old data, so a cut-off date for staff documents and any less important files, dated before 1987, was agreed on, and all those files were stored two floors below ground, with no access by lift.

The rooms had been wired for electricity, but the several 40watt bulbs barely gave out enough light to read anything. Majid had been down here only once in the ten years of his employment, and he always told himself he would not make the same mistake twice should he have to revisit the vaults. He held the torch firmly in one hand and shone it on one of the rows of archive boxes marked A - F, then the next row marked G - M.

Luckily the box marked G was within reach. Any higher and he would have had a wasted journey. He placed the box on the floor and opened it. There had not been many employees with a surname beginning with H.

Hussain. N.A. 1972 - 1992
Hafeez G.M   1928 - 1940
Holland. D   1977 - 1981

There it was: Holland.D. Record of Employment. Staff No. 134/12.

Majid placed the torch on the shelf facing him and opened the file. There was little-written content but a lot of dust.

Name: Dianne Holland
Age: no entry
Married: no entry
Previous employment:
Paris. Musée National des Arts   Asiatiques- Guimet
Education: Leicester University, England
Department: Ceramics
Start Date: February 12th 1977
Leaving Date: April 10th 1981
Address:
Comments: Good worker this lady is.
Forwarding information: ASI New Delhi

Majid took the file and folded it carefully, placing it in his jacket pocket, and returned the archive box to the shelf. Now to climb back up to daylight and clean air.

Once back in his office he scanned the single sheet of paper and emailed Mr J. Lacey, Solicitor, with the information he has asked for, and pondered again on the reward that would surely be forthcoming, for finding the lady to whom an inheritance is due, and be able to buy the best and most comfortable calipers available.

Chapter Eleven

Dear Mr Lacey

In reply to your email of the 22nd, I am pleased to inform you that our museum did employ a person of that name, D Holland, between 1977 and 1981.

I have attached a copy of the employment record and hope this will be of use in finding her. Please contact me if I can be of further assistance. If a financial reward is available please send it to me at the address below.

Regards
Majid Patel, Administrator
Taxila Museum

I read the email again. YES! I called out and then looked around to see if I was alone. Fortunately, I was. I called Jonathan.

"I have had a reply from that museum in Rawalpindi. She worked there for four years and then it says here she went to something called the ASI in New Delhi, whatever that is."

"That's a good lead James, excellent. Do you want me to make enquiries?"

"Thanks, but I will pick it up from here. I need to keep on this now I have something positive. Are you still OK for lunch?"

"Of course, James. See you there."

I should have called Jayne but I needed to press on with this lead. So, she was in Pakistan from 1977 at one museum, and then went to India for nearly ten years, 1981 until 1992. So where does Seoul come into the equation? She must have made an impression in that time. Someone must remember a European lady who worked there for that length of time. I suddenly felt a renewed energy. Jayne was right. It only needed one small clue to spur me on. There was no need to follow the Cairo lead anymore. We now know she worked in Pakistan, and then in India, so that is where I must go. "Go!"

Did I say go? I meant call, didn't I? Flying around Europe is one thing, but Asia . . . that's different. I would need to be very sure of my facts to consider going over there, and if I had the facts, why would I need to go anyway?

An enigma lay before me. Was something drawing me to Asia?

Mother still keeps in touch by letter with her relations, as nani can no longer write, and I am sure she would go and visit if she really wanted to. Money is not the issue, so what is?

I stood up and stretched, clearing my head of these distractions. I noticed Mr Wicks was in early. I still had an issue with the conversation we had had recently and I felt sure he was holding back on something. The phone rang, bringing me back to the present. It was a client for Mr Morris and I transferred the call.

. . .

Lunch with Jonathan was predictable. Two pints of Pride and a green Thai curry for him. One pint of shandy and a Khao man kai for me.

"So, James, you are in a better mood, having had some good news."

"I suppose I am really. Yesterday I did feel like chucking the whole lot in and telling Michael Parker we had hit a brick wall."

"Glad you didn't, James. It's been a good distraction for me too. I like this detective lark."

"Hey, I am a solicitor, supposedly. That's what I trained for and one day hope to be a partner. I am NOT a detective, Jonathan."

"I know that, but it has been interesting, you have to admit. Look where you have been in the last two months, Ireland, France, and now possibly Pakistan and India," he said beaming.

"That's not going to happen. I can do everything by phone and bring this to a swift conclusion." I said, trying to convince myself that is what will happen.

"What does the client want James. Have you considered that?"

In truth, no I have not, and why should I? He is reliant on my reports and evidence and recommendations. That should be enough.

That evening I brought Jayne up-to-date with developments, and she agreed the Cairo connection was probably not relevant now. She saw I was looking forlorn again.

"I thought you would be excited, especially with the news from Pakistan," she said.

"I know, but it's too early to celebrate. I still have no positive ID of her in India yet."

Jayne frowned at me, trying to make me feel guilty.

"Don't look at me like that. It is coming together . . . slowly . . . maybe . . . it's just that I don't want to make assumptions, or plans, before we have all the facts . . ."

She pounced. "Plans! What plans, James?"

Why do I always get this part wrong? "I was thinking ahead to if we do track our Dianne Holland down, wherever she may be, Parker will want me to see her in person to deliver his letter, and that could be Europe, Asia, even America, I don't know." I said shrugging.

We were quiet for a while, considering - no, respecting each other's point of view I guess. Jetting around Europe with Jayne has been fun and she has certainly been helpful, but further afield, well, that's different. To go to Asia together would put my relationship with Michael Parker on a different footing. He entrusted me with his secret, and now at least five other people know of its existence; Jayne, Jonathan, Mr Morris, mother and Mr Wicks. Goodness knows who else has picked up on it. Have I betrayed my client's confidentiality? Morris needed to know, but the others I am not so sure about. On the other hand, I would probably not know what I do without Jonathan or Jayne's help. I looked at Jayne and held her hand. "I am sorry. I value your help, and you have been wonderful and understanding and . . ." She pulled me towards her and we kissed. "I love you," I whispered. "I love you too, James Lacey, and if you have to go further afield to find this woman, then so be it." We kissed again. "But," she said locking eyes, "you had better not make a habit of it. A girl can get lonely."

. . .

The following morning I got to the office early, as I wanted to do some research on this ASI place.

I keyed in ASI New Delhi, and there it was, The Archaeological Survey of India, with its headquarters in New Delhi. It's a vast organization, overseeing hundreds of regional museums and archaeological sites all over the country – no wonder Dianne was drawn there.

The "contacts" page on the website was very comprehensive, listing over twenty names with their positions, emails address and telephone number. I thought of emailing, but I was now impatient for news, so I decided to telephone. All the contacts where prominent heads of department, but no one from Human Resources, so I opted for the switchboard number.

The line rang, and rang, but was eventually answered. "Do you speak English please?" I asked the lady who had rattled off her welcoming speech in Urdu.

"Yes, of course," she replied in perfect English.

"I am calling from London and would like to speak to someone in HR about a member of staff who worked for the ASI in 1981."

The line went quiet. I thought she had cut me off. (No waiting music).

"Hello." A lady's voice suddenly asked. "Who are you?"

"My name is James Lacey. I am a solicitor in London and wondered if anyone could give me information on an English lady who worked at the museum between 1981 and 1992."

"That will take some time, Mr Lacey. Please can you email me with the information you want so I have all the facts? Why are you looking for this person?"

A good question. "She may be entitled to part of an inheritance from a relative." I lied, but maybe not. I still had no idea what Michael Parker's intentions towards her were.

I emailed the lady I had spoken to, Mrs Ali, with an official request from my office for any information on where Dianne Holland may have moved to after leaving India. I was in for a long wait. After four days I emailed again, and again after a week. On the fourteenth day I telephoned.

"I am sorry, Mr Lacey. Your request is being dealt with by one of our Heads of Department, Professor Siddiqui-Chaudhary."

"Well, may I speak to him please?" Silence. "I am sorry, he is not in today. I will remind him to respond to your request."

That was now two weeks ago. Then suddenly I received a very short email.

"Dear Mr Lacey

I am sorry to inform you we have no information to part with on your request for Dianne Holland.

Kind regards

Prof Mohammad Rafi Siddiqui-Chaudhary"

I read the email again. No information to part with. What the hell does that mean? They have some information but don't want to part with it, or they have no information – perhaps the meaning was lost in translation.

Why, after four weeks they suddenly say they have no information. Why did it take so long? The more I thought about it the more it troubled me.

I decided to consult with Jonathan. "Well, we know one thing for sure my friend."

"And what is that?"

"Your Dianne Holland was in India for at least six years in New Delhi. If she was not, they would have said outright – not have a Professor, a department head, write in person trying to put you off the scent."

"Is that what you think, he doesn't want to acknowledge she was there or . . . is protecting her." I thought about this. "But would anyone still know her from the mid-eighties, she would have been around forty-two then. If someone there was near the same age that would make them in their late seventies. What are the chances of a seventy-year-old Professor still working at the museum?" I then remembered de La Lodge in Paris. He must have been well into his seventies.

Jonathan looked at me and smirked.

"Oh, no," I said, putting my hands up in mock self-defense. "I can read your mind, and it's not pleasant."

"So are you going to tell her, or do you want me to . . . mine's a pint."

PART TWO

Chapter Twelve

Martin Sterne was twenty-two in 1965 when he first came to London to study Law, having spent the previous two years at Harvard. He was what you would call a studious fellow - a book-worm. Loved reading Law, the classics, poetry and viewing the Pre-Raphaelite painters of the mid-19th century, Dante in particular. He was also a loner, preferring his own company, or that of interesting historical individuals.

Whilst at college in London studying for his Graduate Diploma in Law, he rented a flat in Holland Park. It was on the top floor of an early Victorian semi-detached house, on a corner plot. The rooms were large, with high ceilings and wide sash windows which let in copious amounts of a cool breeze on a hot summer's evening.

Not only the sounds of London poured in through the open windows, but the sounds of passion and lovemaking that seemed to invade his every waking moment during that summer, from the rooms below him - the rooms where Michael and Dianne lay, and loved.

Sterne had met Michael Parker a few times, usually in the hallway or on the stairs, and they generally nodded to each other. One Saturday in July, Martin was talked into throwing a party, to celebrate the end of year one studies by his friends. The sounds of the 60's played out across Holland Park that evening and everyone was happy and high.

Well, almost everyone. Michael Parker was not a fan of popular music, preferring the more poetic references of James Taylor and Leonard Cohen. "Damn that noise," he shouted across the room to Dianne. "Oh come on, lover. It's a party. You can't dance to Cohen." Dianne shouted back. Michael considered that comment momentarily but just shrugged, thinking, 'why would you'.

"We have been invited and I want to go. Come on. You will enjoy it," she said, brushing her auburn shoulder-length hair.

"If you want to, then fine. I will go for an hour. Perhaps I can sabotage the record player."

"Don't you dare," she said laughing, zipping up her new bright green polka-dot mini dress.

Young Sterne was with a girl he had taken to the cinema a few times but had not slept with her. She was going to drop him after the party if she could not get into bed with him - "life's too short to wait to be asked," was the motto of the time, and she wanted it. Not that Martin was particularly good looking, but he had intellect, and money.

The door of the flat was open, and there were bodies everywhere. Michael and Dianne climbed over several to get to the kitchen, and found some clean wine glasses. "Hi, Di." Pamela called from the kitchen door. Pamela was from Melbourne and travelling around Europe, and had a room on the ground floor. Michael had met her a couple of times and instantly took a dislike to her.

"Hi, Mickey," that was one reason, "how the hell are you sport?"

"Fine thanks, Pamela. Still here then. What happened to Europe?"

"It's not going anywhere soon, so no worries mate. Anyway, I would miss my beautiful Di," she said, giving a Dianne a long firm hug, finishing with a kiss on the cheek.

"Let me know when you get fed up with this wallaby," she whispered loud enough for Michael to hear.

Michael took Dianne's hand and pulled her closer, away from the Aussie lesbian (that was the other reason). "How about that dance you promised."

The mood was slow now, approaching midnight, and they danced to Mr. Tambourine Man and I Got You Babe, before collapsing on the spot with heat exhaustion.

Martin Sterne was weary of the noise, and his friends, who had drunk everything in sight, and was now looking for an excuse to leave his own flat. He saw the young couple slumped on the floor. The green mini dress inching higher around her slender thighs. Michael Parker wearily raised his head and saw Sterne standing over them.

"You must be Michael," Sterne said, offering his hand. "Yes," Michael replied slowly, thinking Sterne was offering to help him up from the floor, but pulled on the outstretched hand, which brought Sterne to the floor, on top of them both.

"Hey, watch the tights," Dianne complained, pushing Sterne off of her.

"Sorry, I didn't mean to do that," Sterne said apologetically, inches from Dianne's face.

"I think we need some fresh air," he said, glancing over to Michael.

"Good idea," Michael agreed, "how about coming down to our ... her ... flat for a drink," he suggested, trying not to breathe in too much of the passive mind-blowing smog. All three helped each other up and made their way out of the room, and down the stairs to Dianne's flat.

"Hey," came a loud cry, "where are you guys off to so early?" the Aussie asked. "Can I come?" she added as an afterthought, hoping for some mischief.

Michael looked at Dianne as if to say "no bloody way," but Dianne just raised her arm and indicated for Pamela to join them.

"She's harmless," Dianne whispered, don't be jealous," and kissed him to prove a point, just as Pamela caught up with them.

"Hey lover, save some for me," she said, winking at Michael, who was not amused. "Only joking, Di . . . unfortunately," she added, blowing Dianne a kiss and continuing into the flat.

The noise had subsided, but not the heat. Even though the windows were open the air was still and heavy. It was midnight on midsummer's day - a fact that had not gone unnoticed by Pamela.

"Hey, aren't we supposed to dance naked around some stones at midnight?" she asked, flicking through the few LP's Dianne had lying around.

"I think they're playing in Plymouth tonight, so maybe not," Martin said, in all seriousness. Everyone looked at him with a puzzled expression, and then Michael laughed, followed by Dianne. "Very funny. Good one." Michael said, pointing at Sterne.

"What's funny?" Pamela wanted to know.

"Don't tell," Michael suggested, "let her work it out." This did not go down well with Pamela.

"How about a drink?" Michael suggested. "White wine, Campari or beer."

"Wine please, lover," Pamela called over.

"Yes, same here," Dianne said.

"Want to give me a hand, Martin?" Michael asked, hoping for a quiet word.

Pamela joined Dianne on the two-seater sofa as soon as they were alone. She opened her handbag and took out two rolled joints, offering one to Dianne.

"I'm tempted, but wait until we're alone." Dianne said, nodding towards the kitchen. Pamela touched Dianne's knee and said, "You bet darling, anytime. Just call me," and kissed her cheek.

In the kitchen Michael asked Martin about his girlfriend. "Your lady friend left early."

Martin wiped a glass from the cupboard, before pouring his beer. "Yes, I think she did. Wasn't very keen on her. Not very . . ."

"Intellectual . . ." Michael offered. Martin half smiled. "Am I that transparent?"

"Well, no, but I can see you probably prefer a different type of woman."

Martin acknowledged only by grinning and gave a half shrug, looking at the two women on the sofa in the other room, but one in particular.

"You must have had some wild parties at Harvard . . . plenty of drinking, and smoking the odd dodgy joint." Michael suggested, with a sly grin, hoping to hear some gossip.

Martin glanced at Michael with suspicion, which was instinctive to him. He was really a private person, but that evening had consumed several pints of beer and for some reason felt like sharing. He hardly spoke about his private life or his time in America, which he went to only to please his father, Judge Lawrence Elliot Sterne. In truth, he had few friends, and no one really close enough to confide in. He leant closer to Michael. "Yes, those Harvard boys know how to party. You would be surprised what the professors gave the boys to experiment with, and of course make some pocket money on the side, if you know what I mean."

Michael wasn't too sure, but had a good idea. "So, did you bring back any "souvenirs"? He asked hopefully. Martin sipped the warm beer. "No," he said thoughtfully. "Customs would have been a problem." Hoping Michael would drop the subject. Some secrets should remain secret.

The boys returned with drinks, and Michael played Leonard Cohen, which Pamela said made her feel sick, so reluctantly went back upstairs to re-join the party.

"I think she fancies you," Martin said.

"Bloody dyke," Michael retorted, "she's a trouble maker for sure." The wine was taking its toll, and eventually all three closed their eyes and drifted into a pleasing slumber helped by a haunting melody with lyrics of someone leading them to a river who were wearing rags and feathers . . . but you know you can trust her.

Michael woke about an hour later and instinctively touched his forehead. "Shit," he announced to no one. He looked around him, and indeed no one was there.

"Di," he called out, "are you there?" No answer.

He shuffled slowly to the bedroom and opened the door. Dianne was lying on the bed, fully dressed. "Hey, love. Can you hear me?"

She opened her eyes and blinked several times. "How did I get here? I don't remember."

Her mini dress was riding high, and Michael could see her white panties.

"That bastard. Did he touch you?" Michael was suddenly awake, adrenaline pounding.

"What! What do you mean?" Dianne mumbled, still not fully awake herself.

"That pervert upstairs. He must have carried you in here and . . . God knows."

"Michael, no! He wouldn't. Trust me." Dianne said, taking hold of his hand and making him sit next to her.

"How do you know that? He brought you in here and you would not know what he did."

"I know Martin . . . he wouldn't touch me . . . he respects me too much, I can tell," she said quietly, stroking his hair.

Michael looked around the room, trying to focus. "What do you mean? Has he tried his luck before?" he asked, still not looking at her.

"We haven't spoken that much, but he is very polite and very shy around women. I am surprised he had that party last night, although I think he must have been talked into it," she said, touching Michael's arm.

"He's fine, honest, Michael. It's Pamela I have to watch out for," she smiled, and she pulled him closer. "She's been trying to get into my pants for weeks."

Michael lay beside her and stroked her cheek, and kissed her forehead. "Good job I got in there first then," he whispered and kissed her tenderly on the mouth - his hand sliding her polka-dot mini dress even higher, reaching for those parts Pamela can only ever dream of.

Chapter Thirteen

Jayne was attentive during my analysis at my suggestion to go to India. She nodded in all the right places but remained expressionless, which did worry me. "So," I asked, hunching my shoulders, "what do you think?"

She was sitting opposite me at our gate-leg table. Leaning forward she took hold of my hands and squeezed them gently. "James Lacey, you are the most wonderful, caring, thoughtful guy I have ever known. You could have just told Parker you hit a dead-end and be done with him, but no, you have the will and decency to see this through. I am very proud of you," she managed before a tear trickled down her cheek. I leant over and kissed her. "I love you, Ms Woods," I said, wiping her cheek dry.

"I love you too, Mr Lacey."

We sat in silence for a while longer, taking in the extent of the events before us.

"I need to tell Parker and Morris, and . . . mother." I started reeling off a verbal list of things to do. "Hell, no, not mother, she will want me to take a detour to see her relatives."

"They're your relatives too." Jayne reminded me.

"Yes, I know love, but Cochin is miles from where I am going. Now, I must see if I need jabs, check flights, find a hotel . . . ."

"Hey, slow down, James. You are not going tomorrow. We have time to sort this out," she said, jolting me back to reality.

"Sorry, yes you are right of course. But I must see Parker and tell him about my plans."

. . .

The next day I had to again explain my reasons for wanting to go to India to Mr Morris. There would be no holding of hands or tear-jerking.

"When do you propose to meet with Mr Parker about all of this?" Is all Morris said after my explanation?

"I will call him as soon as we are finished. Are you OK with my analysis, sir? It is the right course of action, I believe."

Mr Morris smiled for what I think was the first time ever since I have worked for him.

"I may seem hard-hearted, James, but I assure you I am as sentimental as the next man. Yes, of course you have made the right decision. Go to India and solve this mystery, for all our sakes."

"Thank you, sir. Thank you very much. I will do my best." And I left his office with a feeling of elation. I was still smiling when I walked back to my office and saw Raj and Mr Wilkes working away.

"Someone looks happy. Had a rise?" Raj asked.

"I wish," but saw Mr Wilkes was looking rather more serious than Raj. "Why don't you get an early lunch Raj. I will look at some of this work with Mr Wilkes." Trying to sound as assertive as I could. Raj jumped at the offer. "And bring me back a Ciabatta sandwich, from the Italian cafe in Bridge Street."

"That's twenty minutes' walk." Raj protested.

"That's fine. Take your time. Have a good walk." And I handed him ten pounds. "Get yours as well out of that."

"Gee, thank James. Are you sure you haven't had a rise," he said, leaving me alone with Mr Wilkes.

Peter Wilkes grinned as I shut the office door and sat down in front of my desk, which he had taken temporary ownership of.

"That was unkind. Making the poor lad walk all that way for you. If I didn't know better, I would think you wanted him out of the way James."

I did indeed want to have a quiet word with Peter Wilkes, but now I was alone with him I was not sure how to approach the subject. "Mr Wilkes..," but before I could say anything he raised his hand. "We have known each other long enough James, and as I am semi-retired please call me Peter."

"Thank you, Peter," I said feeling more relaxed.

"Now, what is it you need to talk about in private?" he asked, with raised eyebrows.

I took a deep breath. "You know I have been doing some ... research, for our client Michael Parker." Peter nodded but said nothing.

"It sounded like a wild-goose chase, to be honest, but over the last couple of months we, that is, I had help from my friend at Frasier & Frasier, and .. my girlfriend, Jayne ... we, err, discovered a lot about the lady I was asked to find, Dianne Holland." Peter blinked a few times as if trying to refocus, just as Sinead had done . . . trying to recall something of importance.

"When we talked briefly a few weeks ago, you seemed to remember the name, but we were interrupted. Do you know the name, sir . . . Peter?" I pressed him. "It may be important."

"It was a long time ago," he finally said quietly, looking directly at me. "Martin Sterne and I shared rented accommodation for a while after we graduated, back in around 1965. It was a small terraced house in Acton."

"Not Holland Park?" I interrupted.

Wilkes blinked again. "No, Acton, I remember it because I could only just afford it. Martin had been in Holland Park before that, but said he did not get on with the other tenants."

I remembered how Michael Parker had mentioned the Australian woman with malice, and of her apparent suicide, and wondered if she was his reason for leaving.

Wilkes continued, breaking my train of thought.

"I was lucky to get an articled clerkship so quickly after graduating, but Martin had to wait three months before finding suitable employment. He was very unsociable during that time. He would go out for hours on end. I asked him one day where did he go? He just said, "Watching and waiting". I had no idea what he meant, but he was always coming out with strange sayings. Liked poetry you know, mostly early stuff . . . what's his name, that painter fellow . . . Dante I think, yes I am sure of it, Dante." He finished, pleased with his recollection of events.

I stared past him at the window. Streaks of sunlight filtered through the Venetian blinds. My mind was also filtering information I could not, dare not, utter.

"Are you OK, James? You look pale."

I smiled at the thought, of looking pale that is. "Yes, I'm fine, thank you.

So what was the connection with Dianne Holland and Mr Sterne?"

"He came home one evening and had obviously been drinking, which was unusual in itself. He could hardly stand. I made him coffee and tried to get him to make sense. Kept going on about how it was his fault she was gone. I asked repeatedly who he was talking about, but he just kept saying the girl downstairs. I think he was in love James, but never had the courage to say anything to her, and then he told me she had left suddenly, and it was too late to do anything about it."

"But how do you know it was Dianne Holland." I insisted.

"Because I found a letter she had written to him. I was not snooping James. I was looking for some journals one day in his room when I saw this letter lying on the floor. It was crumpled as if it had been thrown away, but I retrieved it and smoothed it out again."

"Was there an envelope?" I had to know.

"Not that I recall. Is that important?"

"No." I lied, not wanting him to lose focus. "Can you remember any of the content?"

"Yes, some. It was obviously a love letter. It was headed, My love, and went on to say she was leaving for a while but hoped to return soon, and how she had enjoyed the last few months with him. It was signed Dianne."

How had Martin Sterne been in possession of this letter to Michael? Had Dianne given it to him to pass on to Michael, or . . . the alternative was too unbelievable. I had to see Michael Parker. He deserved to know this. My thoughts were interrupted by the office door swinging open and Raj bursting in. "Hope you are hungry. I am after that long walk."

. . .

I arranged to visit Michael Parker during the week, and had just two days to get my story straight.

He was sitting in the same chair the last time I visited him but looked pale and more sullen than before. "Come in, young man," he continued," what news have you of Dianne."

The room was much the same as I had seen from my previous visit, and I sat opposite him as before. "Well, as you know I thought your original request to find Dianne Holland was going to be a little fanciful, but I must admit we have had some success."

Michael Parker beamed with delight. "Tell me what you have. Where is she?" he asked excitedly.

"Unfortunately we do not know where she is, or if she is alive, Michael. But we do know something that may help you understand why you did not hear from her."

Michael looked pensive as if he was about to be told some solemn secret, which in a way it was.

"It appears Dianne did write to you and left the letter with Pamela, who, as you know died soon after Dianne left, from an overdose I believe you said."

Michael listened, spellbound. "However, I believe, and this is only my personal opinion, the other tenant in the flats may have had something to do with her death, or at the very least, helped her overdose. Why didn't you tell me you knew Martin Sterne from those days?"

Michael reeled back in his chair ignoring my question. "What are you saying? Sterne killed Pamela? But why?"

"He was in love with Dianne and hated Pamela. Somehow he found out about the letter to you Pamela had kept, and thought it was meant for him. It is possible he killed Pamela and made it look like either an overdose or suicide to cover the crime. I am considering doing a search for the police reports into Pamela's death."

Michael stared blankly, not understanding the implications of what he had been told, or so it seemed.

He closed his eyes and shook his head slowly. "All this time she had written a letter I had not seen. But James, what of her and the child if she had one?"

I had to massage the truth a little, until, and if, I ever found Dianne Holland. "We still do not know if she is alive or if she ever had a child. I am afraid that part is still to be uncovered, but we have tracked her movements over the years, and I would like your permission to go to India to visit someone she worked with who may be able to shed further light on the mystery."

Michael looked at me through misty eyes. "Go, my son, and find her. I need to know," and he leant back, exhausted from hearing the truth, and the expectation of what was to come.

. . .

I spent the next few days arranging flights to New Delhi, hotel accommodation and calling the local doctor's surgery to see what jabs I needed, if any. I planned to stay only a few days, but Jayne suggested at least a week, as I am going that far, it seemed a shame not to see something of the country. I was pleased how understanding she was about the whole Michael Parker thing. Not just understanding, but helpful. I would never have got as much information without her. I looked up from my laptop and watched her on the sofa, reading.

"What?" she asked, seeing me staring.

"Nothing. I was thinking about how much I will miss you."

"Come here," she said, putting down her book. I moved over and sat beside her putting my arms around her, and holding her close. We sat in silence for a while, just holding each other. I kissed her forehead. "Are you really OK about me going to India?"

She turned over and put her head in my lap, looking up at me, she stroked my face.

"James, it's the right decision, honestly. I have a feeling you will learn what you need to know to help Parker rest in peace. And yes, I will miss you." And she pulled me down to her lips and we kissed, long and passionately.

. . .

I called Jonathan the next day as I was still concerned about the prospect of Martin Sterne having killed Pamela. We met as usual in the pub.

"Good God, man! An illegitimate child, unofficial adoption – maybe - and now murder. What a story," he beamed, forgetting his pint for a minute.

"Not so loud, Johnny." I said, concerned the whole pub would hear our conversation."

"No worries, James, everyone here is too focused on eating and drinking, which is what we should be doing, but tell me more about the Martin Sterne connection. This is amazing stuff."

I relayed my conversation with Peter Wilkes, and the rest was my judgment of the situation. "What I need to do is get a look at the original police file from 1965. Do you think that is still possible?" I asked, full of doubt.

"Not sure, James, but one other avenue is the press. There must have been a story somewhere."

"Of course," I said a little too loud. "The papers would have had a field day about a tourist found dead in London. Well done Johnny boy that deserves a pint."

Back from the bar, Jonathan was on his mobile. "OK, thanks, Spike, I owe you."

"Who was that?" I inquired.

"That was Spike, an old friend from Uni. He works for Press International, and knows someone in archives but doesn't know how far backstories are kept, or in what format. Back then there were no computers – thank God for progress. Cheers."

"What about the police. Don't suppose you have any old Uni friends in the force?" I asked hopefully.

Jonathan sipped his beer, looking thoughtful. "As it happens, we both know someone," he said with a smile.

"Really? I can't think of anyone . . . unless you mean . . . Oh no, not Samuels, please. He is not a detective for starters, and he is a pain in the backside for another."

"You are too harsh on the man, James. He was helpful last year in finding that missing cat that had been left a fortune by its owner."

"I don't trust him, Jonathan. He nearly screwed that up. Bringing in any cat he found saying it was the one just to get the reward. Totally unprofessional."

"I know, but he did find him in the end, you must admit, and he still knows people in the force who could be very helpful just now."

I cringed at the thought of bringing someone else into the frame, especially Derek Samuels, but Jonathan had a point, he could be useful. "OK," I said, "but you speak to him, and give him only the barest of information, not the whole story. We just want to do some research on an old case, that's all."

"Yes, sir," Jonathan said, saluting. "I will be as discreet as a church mouse."

"I'm not joking. If he gets to hear the full facts God knows what he would do with that kind of information. I am leaving next Wednesday for India, so anything you have by then would be good, otherwise email what you can."

We finished our lunch on a subdued note, and I felt angry with myself for being too hard on Jonathan, but if I was right, and someone else got hold of what we knew, it would be a disaster for all concerned, not least Morris, to learn he had had a murderer in his firm for all those years.

Chapter Fourteen

Jayne drove me to Heathrow Airport on the Wednesday morning for the 9.30am flight to Delhi. We hugged and kissed, and I promised to email every day.

The flight was long, but I took the opportunity to write a synopsis of what I had accomplished so far, and what questions I needed to ask Professor Chaudhary.

I arrived just after midnight and took a taxi to my hotel, where after checking in, crashed out due to jet-lag. I woke the next morning to heavy banging on the door. It was the maid wanting to clean the room. She talked to me in Hindi, expecting me to understand, but soon realized I was not born and bred in India.

After a shower and shave I emailed Jayne to say I had arrived safely, then one to Jonathan asking if he had any updates.

I did not have an appointment with the Professor but felt the need to get there as soon as possible. The taxi driver looked at the address and nodded. I managed to understand it would take around thirty minutes, across the other side of the City.

We drove along the back streets of East Delhi, and crossed over the Yamuan River via the very wide and very busy Nizamuddin Bridge, into the heart of New Delhi. I was captivated by the sights and sounds, especially the sounds – noise everywhere, with cars, lorries, buses, tuc-tuc's and cyclists, all jostling for a piece of the road.

Following the river going north towards the center of town, I saw wide-open spaces, sports stadiums, parks and many large white Temples.

My taxi driver took advantage of my ignorance of the city geography and took me on a sightseeing route, which in hindsight was interesting. We arrived forty-five minutes later outside the ASI building, which shared an entrance with the Indira Gandhi Memorial Museum.

I took a deep breath and entered the air-conditioned reception. The lady behind the reception desk was Ms Urmila Singh, according to her nameplate. "Good morning, Ms. Singh. I am here to see Professor Siddiqui-Chaudhary," hoping my pronunciation was correct and handed her my card.

She looked at me and then the card several times. "Do you have an appointment?" she asked.

"Well, no, not really, but it is of the utmost importance I see the Professor," I said as sincerely as I could.

"This is most unusual. I need to see if he is in today. Please wait here." And she walked hurriedly down the corridor behind her. I sat in the air-conditioned reception area and read the ASI brochure detailing its vast work and responsibilities:

The Archaeological Survey of India (ASI), under the Ministry of Culture, is the premier organization for the archaeological researches and protection of the cultural heritage of the nation. Maintenance of ancient monuments and archaeological sites and remains of national importance is the prime concern of the ASI. For the maintenance of ancient monuments and archaeological sites and remains of national importance the entire country is divided into 24 Circles. The organization has a large workforce of trained archaeologists, conservators, epigraphist, architects and scientists for conducting archaeological research projects through its Circles, Museums, Excavation Branches, Prehistory Branch, Epigraphy Branches, Science Branch, Horticulture Branch, Building Survey Project, Temple Survey Projects and Underwater Archaeology Wing.

I could see why Dianne would have found this particular posting of interest. Such a wide scope of opportunity, and to work with many people in the same field must have been rewarding and stimulating.

Ms Singh found the Professor in his usual spot in the atrium garden, sitting and reading in the shade of a large coconut tree.

"Professor, there is a gentleman here asking for you. I think he is from England. This is his card."

The Professor read the card and sighed, shaking his head. "No, no, no. He must not be here," he whispered, partly to himself, but Ms Singh could see he was perplexed by this news. "What shall I tell him, Professor?"

"Tell him I am not here, Ms Singh. I am never here, do you understand?" He said, holding her arm, not tightly, but enough for her to realize he was serious. She nodded she understood and returned to the reception.

I stood as soon as she came into sight, but I could not read her expression, but soon discovered her answer. "I am sorry, Mr Lacey, the

Professor is not in today, and no one seems to know when he will be back. He is partly retired you see," she said, sounding baffled, and not looking at me directly.

I was afraid of this. He must be in his seventies by now. I tried another approach.

"He has been in recently as he emailed me with some information I asked for. Perhaps I can visit his home." I suggested, with some optimism.

Ms Singh was shaking her head. "I am sorry. We cannot give out that information. If you leave me your hotel address or phone number I will see what I can do, that is all I can promise. I am sorry."

I wrote my mobile number on the back of my card, with the hotel name, but did not have their number with me. "Please see if you can get a message to him. It is very important I see him, for my clients' sake." And handed her my card, and nodded my appreciation before leaving.

Ms Singh handed the Professor James's card again. "He said it was important he speak with you, sir, "for his client's sake." She waited for a response, but he just stared into space, hoping he had made the right decision. Just as Ms Singh turned to leave, he reached out to her and held her arm again. "Please, Urmila, he is not to see me, ever. If he calls again please persuade him to leave. That is all I can say." She nodded her understanding, and left him with his thoughts, wondering what the great mystery was all about.

I walked out into the blistering heat, and the noise, which brought me back to reality. Not knowing where to go, I found myself at the gates of the Indira Gandhi Memorial Museum and followed a group of visitors through to the main entrance. The grounds are extensive, and peaceful, as they should be. Peacocks displayed their colorful palette of feathers, and modern statues adorned the lawns. I learnt from walking through the museum this was actually Gandhi's house, and was turned into a museum after her assassination in 1984.

I look at these institutions now with renewed interest ever since Michael Parker sent me on his quest. They are, after all, our heritage, and if it were not for the likes of Dianne Holland and all who went before her, and since, we would not have wondrous collections of fine art, ceramics, books, glass and textiles, and everything else that are housed in these palaces of reflection.

After a welcome cool drink in the adjoining cafe, I hailed a taxi back to my hotel to plan my next move.

I checked my iPad for messages. One from Jayne saying how she is missing me and one from Jonathan saying he had no news on "you know what". At least he is taking this seriously.

I was sure the Professor was somewhere in the ASI building. I decided to return in the morning and press Ms Singh harder or speak to someone in HR. I could not have come all this way on a wild goose chase, could I?

The next morning after breakfast I took a taxi to the ASI building again. This time it took twenty-five minutes and saved me three pounds. Ms Singh was in her usual place and looked taken aback when she saw me standing over her.

"Mr Lacey, I did not expect you back. I said we will call you if we have any information."

"I know, and I am sorry to be insistent, but I do not have long here, and my client also has very little time," I said, without dwelling on Michael Parker's terminal fate.

"What can I do? I have already said the Professor is not here."

"I know, but can someone else help? Maybe someone in HR or a similar department, ceramics I believe." I said, leaning over the desk to impress on her how earnest I was.

"Wait here," she said, and started walking down the same corridor as yesterday. Soon she was out of sight, having turned right at the end. I paced the small entrance area, feeling impatient. After five minutes my impatience got the better of me and I traced her footsteps along the corridor in search of her, or whoever she was talking to. I spied her a few yards ahead, having turned right into an elegant walkway, being one side of a garden quadrangle.

She was talking to an elderly gentleman, dressed in traditional Indian garments, a colorful dhoti and white kurta shirt.

I approached slowly, hoping to hear some conversation, but realized, of course, they were speaking Hindi. The gentleman saw me first, and Ms Singh turned abruptly. "Mr Lacey, please, you are not allowed back here." And proceeded to escort me back. I stood my ground.

"I am sorry, but I really must insist on seeing the Professor. Is this he?" I said, looking in the man's direction. Ms Sing was about to say something when the man came forward and spoke in perfect English.

"I understand you are looking for Rafi, that is Professor Siddiqui-Chaudhary," he said with a smile. "I am sorry but he is not in today." And turned to Ms Singh who was now looking confused. "It's OK, Urmila, I will talk to this gentleman now. You can leave us." And with that Ms Singh returned, relieved of the responsibility, to her post.

"Ms Singh tells me you need to meet with Rafi, sorry, that is what he is known by to everyone here."

"Yes, I have written previously but I did not get a full reply to the information I asked for," I explained.

"So, you came here, to India, especially to meet with Rafi, not knowing if he was here at all?"

"I know it sounds crazy, but yes, that just about sums it up. The person we are looking for may be entitled to an inheritance." I lied again. "May I ask your name, Sir?"

"Sorry, of course, Rajeev Sharma, a friend and colleague of Rafi's." He said without hesitation. "How long are you here for?"

Until next Wednesday, then I return to London."

"Ah, I see. And you are staying nearby, or with relatives. I assume you have Asian bloodline."

I hadn't thought about my relatives. They were many miles away in Kerala. "I am in a hotel on the other side of town, but yes, my mother's family was originally from Kerala. My grandmother came to England in 1946, but I have only visited once when I was six."

"Ah yes, many families split. Many lives lost," he said, nodding and shaking his head as is the custom when speaking over here. His eyes then opened wide. "But you must visit them, yes, while you are here. You have time to spend with them. It will be good for you."

I hardly had time to understand what he was suggesting when he took me by the arm and started walking to the opposite end of the courtyard, into an office. His name, Rajeev Sharma, was on the door. "Sit down . . . James, is it, can I call you James?"

"Yes please, but what are you suggesting."

"Rafi will be back on Monday, so you have all weekend to visit your relations, yes. There is a flight to Cochin I am sure this afternoon. I can arrange a taxi." And he started to dial a number. Then he had another thought. "James, do you have many clothes, kurtas and dhoits?

You will need something more Indian I think. Your western clothes will be very hot down there," he said, with a flourish of hand waving, forgetting he was holding the phone.

"I only have a few shirts and a couple of pairs of trousers, a jacket and tie, and ..."

"No, no, you need more comfortable clothes for visiting. We will call into my cousin's shop on the way to the airport, and you can have some kurtas and dhotis and pajamas. Leave it to me, I will call him now to expect us."

I could not keep up with him. At first, he seemed like a sheepish old man, and then the next minute he was superman, full of energy. I did not know how to tell him I had no idea where my relatives lived, but if I was going I could phone mother. At least she would be pleased. But was this a distraction? Was I being manipulated? Why couldn't Mr Sharma just tell me where the Professor was?

"Mr Sharma, I appreciate your kind offer and consideration, but this is not necessary. Can you tell me where the Professor lives and I can visit him over the weekend? Perhaps you can introduce me to him."

With head-nodding, he replaced the receiver. "I am sorry, James. I was only trying to help you trace your roots, as you are here. Rafi is out of town this weekend. He often visits his family in Jodhpur.

If you prefer to spend the weekend in your hotel, or sightseeing then that is also good, of course," he said smiling and sounding very persuasive.

I clenched my teeth and nodded in surrender. "I am sorry, you are right. It would be good to visit, but I have to go back to the hotel and get my case."

"Yes, yes, of course. We can stop off on the way to the airport from my cousin's shop, which is not far." And picked up the phone again and spoke, I assume, to his cousin. After that call, he phoned the airport to check flight times. "Good, there is a flight at two this afternoon, arriving at eight. I will reserve you a seat, with a return flight on Monday evening." And with that done, he whisked me into a taxi and headed to his cousin's shop.

In the taxi I texted mother asking for uncle Jogin's number, explaining what I was up to, but without the theatricals. As the UK is six hours behind India I did not expect an answer for another three or four hours. I also texted Jayne and told her the same story.

I knew she would be pleased, and promised to email her later, and explain what is really happening to me.

Mr Sharma's cousin's shop was a vast mix of haberdashery and colorful garments for men, women and children. Not particularly on the tourist trail, but offering a good range of services to both the public and tourist. It seems Mr Sharma had called ahead and ordered several articles of clothing for me, in various sizes to save time. He insisted I stayed in the taxi while he collected the garments. We then drove to my hotel where I repacked the newly acquired wardrobe, passport, money and toiletries, and prayed I had not forgotten anything. While I was doing all of that, Mr Sharma said he would explain to the receptionist that I will be away for a couple of days, returning sometime Monday.

On the final leg of the journey to the airport, I had time to reflect on the past two hours activities. "I must pay you for the shirts. How much do I owe you?"

"Nothing my boy, it's all taken care of. After all, I insisted you have some new clothes so I am responsible for them."

"That is very generous of you, but I really think I need to pay something."

"Not another word, James, we are nearly there. Do call in when you get back, won't you."

We shook hands outside the terminal, and he was back in the taxi and disappeared like a whirlwind. I collected my tickets and filled in copious amounts of forms just because I was a "foreigner" on an internal flight. I slept most of the flight and arrived at Cochin Airport with a certain amount of trepidation. I checked my phone for messages but there was nothing from mother, so I had no idea where I was going. I walked out of immigration into a sea of a thousand faces, all searching for someone familiar who had exited the customs hall. I glanced around the throng of faces, not expecting to see anyone I recognized, but then suddenly saw a large card held aloft with a hand-written name on it: JAMES SHARJEEL

Chapter Fifteen

After Professor Chaudhary returned to the ASI offices, he went directly to his own desk in the office he shares with his colleague Rajeev Sharma. He turned on the computer and sent an email. *My dear Lady Grey . . .*

. . .

I waved my arm towards the man holding the card. "Hello, I am James."

"Yes, of course, you are. I am Joji. You probably do not recognize me," he said, reaching out with his right hand. We shook hands and we looked each other up and down. Joji is my Grandmother's sister's son. The last time I saw him he was twenty-seven and getting married.

"You were about five when you came over for my wedding."

"Yes, I remember some of it. Especially how hot it was. How is everyone? I hope I am not intruding. It is a very short stop-over. I am . . ."

"Hey, it's fine James. Let's get you back and you can tell me on the way."

We made our way through the throbbing crowds and headed for the car park. "Is it always this crowded?" I asked, slightly bewildered by the size of the crowds.

"Yes, this is a very busy airport. I come here nearly every day. I have a taxi business."

"How far do you live from here, Joji?"

We had found his car, a Honda Civic, and stowed my overnight case in the boot.

"About forty minutes in this traffic."

"I am sorry to spring this on you after not seeing you for so long."

"Its fine, I promise. Everyone is looking forward to seeing you. Fiya and the children will be there, and your aunt Gini and uncle Jogin as well. They live with us."

I leant back in my seat and sighed. "I don't know what they will think of me. I have come without anything. Can we stop off and buy something? Sweets, flowers, anything. What do I take to people I don't know?" I asked feeling exasperated.

"Don't worry, James. We need to get back for dinner. As soon as your mother called, amma has been running around like a mad dog, making a welcoming meal. And for someone of seventy-eight, that's not bad," he smiled. Come to think of it, he had not stopped smiling since we met.

I did not know a lot about my relatives, which put me at a disadvantage. My grandparents, Sami and Jamilah Sharjeel, moved to England in 1946 fearing what was to come after Partition. Their family, however, were of mixed caste and many of their lineage married into European families. Why my grandparents were fearful of a backlash of religious segregation I was never really sure about, as they were not Muslim or Hindu, and my mother says she neither could find the true reason for them settling in the UK.

I noticed immediately, however, Joji, and presumably, his family were Christians, as he openly displayed a crucifix and a faded picture of Jesus on the dashboard.

I had learnt that Kerala has a very high population of Catholic Christians, almost equaling the Muslim inhabitants. This was going to be an education as well as a baptism by fire.

As soon as we arrived everyone came out to meet us. Most were speaking in what I thought was Hindi. "I am sorry Joji, I cannot understand Hindi."

"No matter. The main language here is Malayalam, or English, so you will be OK," he said, still smiling.

"James, you must be James. Let me see you my boy." An elderly woman with neat grey hair and a wrinkled complexion stood directly in front of me. "You have your mother's eyes . . . but that is about all. Give your auntie Gini a hug." We hugged and she kissed me.

"Give the boy some air amma . . ." Joji said, sensing my apprehension. "He has had a long journey. Let's all go in and we can do the introductions there."

The house was large, by most standards, and I, like many westerners pre-judged how the average Indian lives. My relatives seem to have done OK for themselves.

"James, this is my wife Fiya," Joji explained, and I greeted her with a traditional hand greeting, palms together. "Hello, James," she said and kissed me on each cheek. "It is good to meet at last. I have heard a lot about you."

"Oh . . . I hope not too much." I said, trying to sound casual, but not succeeding.

"Come and meet muthappa, your uncle Jogin."   Uncle Jogin was seated in a high-backed chair and smiled as we approached, holding out his right hand.

"Good to meet you, James. I am sorry we have not seen your family for a time. I hope you can stay longer next time."

"I hope so as well. Mother has always wanted to come back, but your sister-in-law does not travel far now."

I said, trying to defend why no one had met each other for twenty-one years. Uncle Jogin nodded and looked away at the mention of Grandmas name.

"Come, James," Joji said, pulling me aside. I want you to meet my children. This is Geon, he is nineteen, and this is our daughter Mayz."

We kissed and shook hands where appropriate. "Finally, this is my sister Gigitta and her husband George, and their son, Rayyan. They have come over from Cochin to see you."

"I am sorry." I started to say.

"Nonsense, we are all very fascinated to meet you and want to know everything about you and your wife," Mayz said, taking my arm and leading me to a large sofa.

. . .

Jonathan had called their mutual friend Samuels and briefed him about some information he needed for a client.

"That will cost you, considering how you treated me the last time we did business."

"You stepped out of line Samuels, and you know it. Now if you don't want this then I can find someone else," and was poised to put down the phone."

"Don't bluff a bluffer Johnny boy. You only called me because you have no one else, right."

Jonathan considered hanging up regardless but knew he needed someone with inside knowledge. "OK, but if you screw this up, I will see you are finished. Am I clear?"

"Perfectly. Now, what the hell do you want that no one else can get you?"

. . .

"Married! Why do think I am married?" I asked.

"Take no notice of her, James. Mayz, behave," and her father continued in his own language, and from the expression on his daughter's face, she was looking sheepish.

"Sorry, James," Joji said. "It was just a way of seeing if you are married."

"She only had to ask." I said, still confused.

"Yes, but that would have been too easy for her," he said, shooting another stern look at his daughter.

Everyone was looking at me now, seven smiling faces, all wanting a piece of me. The 'relative' from England. The stranger in their family. Hell, I knew this was a mistake.

"Enough, all of you. Leave the poor boy alone and come and eat. The meal is ready. Come, James, we can talk while we eat, and you can tell us how you came to be here today." Auntie Gini said as she ushered everyone into the dining room. "I did not have time to prepare a Saday, but maybe tomorrow, or before you leave."

"That would be lovely. Your sister made them when I was younger, but we do not have them so much now."

The table was covered with brightly colored dishes. I recognized the fish curry and the biryani, but there were many other interesting dishes I was looking forward to trying. It is well known that Indian cuisine, especially in the south, has no bearing on what we have in restaurants in the UK. The closest would be if it was cooked at home, like mother and grandmother cook sometimes.

"So, James," Uncle Jogin asked from across the table, "why are you in India?"

Everyone stopped eating and turned to me for my answer. "Well, it's a long story . . ."

"That's OK, we have all night, and tomorrow is Saturday so I don't have to work," Mayz said, winking at me.

Geon came to my rescue. "Sister, leave him alone and let him speak." I smiled back at everyone. It was getting contagious this smiling.

"Well, my firm of solicitors was asked by one of its oldest clients to trace someone for him. I was available, so it fell to me to visit this client one day and he told me he was dying and wanted to find someone he had known, a lady, from forty years ago."

I had a captive audience. However, I was hungry and continued to eat the wonderful meen curry. Others sat, absorbed. "Go on," Joji said, "have you found her?"

"No, not exactly. We know she was an archaeologist and worked in many countries, France, Egypt, Korea, Pakistan and India. That is why I am here. I visited the offices in New Delhi to speak with a colleague but he is not back until Monday or Tuesday, so I thought I could kill two birds with one stone … if you know what I mean, and … well I was here anyway."

"No matter the reason, James, it is good you are here. We will make you welcome and show you some of our lovely Kerala in the short time you are here." Joji said, and everyone nodded in agreement.

. . .

Samuels spent one wet afternoon at the police archives in Kew, near London, looking for the case files of Pamela Norton. He found reference to the case file quickly via the computer terminal in the research room. However, the case file was marked "closed" for one hundred years. Sealed until 2065.

"Damn. Why on earth was this one sensitive?" Samuels mused, and then smiled to himself. This assignment might prove more lucrative than he first thought.

Just because a case file was marked "closed" did not mean it could not be accessed - the Freedom of Information Act was not around in 1965. However, if Samuels put in an official request to see the file and it was refused, it would make it more difficult to get to it via any other means. The only sure way to see its content was to have a senior officer request access - and he knew just the person to ask.

. . .

"You must be tired, James," Gigitta asked.

"Yes, a little. It has been a long, but interesting day," I said looking around the room wondering where I was to sleep.

The ladies cleared away the table and Joji beckoned me to join him on the sofa. Geon sat nearby with Rayyan. "So," I asked, "Geon, what do you do?"

"I am at the Naval College in Cochin for another two years studying engineering," he answered with a smile.

"Oh, you are joining the Navy?"

"No. I managed to get a placement at the college. It's nothing to do with joining the Navy. They run it as an external education system."

"He is doing well. I am very proud of him," his father stated.

"And what about you Rayyan. Are you at college?"

"I am finishing my last year at law school. I will be a Lawyer like you," he beamed proudly. "I would very much like to talk to you about some aspects of English Law compared with our system and . . ."

"Rayyan. Enough. James is tired. It can wait until another time." His father interrupted.

"It's OK, but perhaps we can keep in touch via email, and I will help if I can." Hoping that would be acceptable for the time being.

Just then Gigitta brought in a tray of sweets and tea. "I hope you like Cardamom tea, James."

"I do. Grandma makes it often." I said, relishing the taste of this wonderful elixir.

We sat and talked for another hour or so, bringing them up to date with mother's move to Solihull, and grandfather not being too well. I noticed aunt Gini looking very concerned whenever I mentioned grandfather's name. "What is wrong with him James? Is he in hospital? She asked, thoughtfully."

"No, not when I left. I think it's just old age I am afraid, auntie. He is frail now and stays mostly in bed."

Auntie Gini looked away and nodded slowly, either confirming my diagnosis or remembering something else.

"James." Joji suddenly called out. I refocused. "Yes, Joji."

"How would you like to get up very early and see the sunrise?"

"No father!" Mayz called over, followed by similar gasps of shock from other family members. "That's not fair, Joji." His mother stated firmly. "I hope you are not thinking of Kolukkumalai . . ."

"No, no. That's too far, but I know somewhere closer that has just as good a view. Perhaps Idamalayar. It's only about an hour away, and I am sure James will not have seen such a wonderful sunrise as there."

I sat wondering what to say. "What time are we talking about?" I asked casually.

"We will leave here at 4.30am. That will give us time to reach the highest point across the reservoir." And without drawing breath turned to his wife." We will need a flask of tea and some breakfast."

"Just us?" I asked out of interest, looking around the room.

"No, we have all seen it before - several times," Geon said, but adding an afterthought for my benefit, "it is worth going, once."

. . .

DCI Zoe Canton opened the door wearing civvies. Jeans and a ribbed cotton tank-top.

"Hi, Zoe. You still look gorgeous. Even at your age." Samuels came straight out with his usual compliment.

"You prick, Samuels. Your chat-up has not improved over time," she replied, stony-faced. "What favor are you asking from me this time?"

"How suspicious. I could have called just to wish you a happy birthday."

"That was two months ago and you know it. Try again." Samuels looked dejected.

"OK," he frowned. "I'll come clean. I need a favor. I do bring gifts, however," and brought from behind his back a bottle of vodka and a box of Belgian chocolates."

"You bribing me, Samuels? I could arrest you for that."

"Can we dispense with the foreplay, it's getting cold out here."

DCI Zoe Canton opened the door wider and gestured Samuels to come indoors.

"You've decorated since my last visit. Very nice," he said approvingly.

"Cut the crap and tell me what you want."

"Drink for a start my love, and chill-out. You are very uptight."

Zoe poured two large vodkas and added a splash of tonic water. "Ice?" she asked.

"No thanks, I'm cold enough."

Samuels sat on the large corner sofa. Zoe passed him his drink and sat opposite. "Hey, come and sit next to me like you used to," he insisted.

"Behave, Samuels, all that is over. Get to the point." Zoe said calmly, sipping her drink.

Samuels sighed and cocked his head looking dejected, but he had expected nothing less. DC Zoe Canton, as she was then, ten years ago, and Samuels had had a brief but satisfying affair. Well technically, she had the affair as she was married. Samuels had never been married and vowed he never would be. He valued his independence too much. He was old school - not caring too much for women's lib. Zoe had risen to DCI soon after and broke off the affair, saying it was now too dangerous - she had responsibilities to the job and her husband. Samuels understood - always more fish in the sea - but never let Zoe forget he could damage her if he ever wanted to. He never would of course. He did have some feelings left, and a few scruples, but he would never admit it to anyone.

"Alright, I have a cold case. I'm working for a solicitor and his side-kick. They want some info on a closed file." Samuels delved into his inside coat pocket and handed Zoe a piece of paper. "This is the case file number I found at Kew. It's locked until 2065. The case was in 1965"

"One hundred years. Must have been sensitive." Zoe was interested now. "Do we know who was involved? Was there a victim?"

Samuels smiled. She was going to do just fine. He filled her in on the background as much as he had been told. "I still don't know why they want to see the file. New evidence may be. Who knows, but files can be obtained on new evidence can't they?"

Zoe leant back in her chair. "OK, I'll see what I can do. But on one condition only, Samuels, you never come here again."

. . .

The sleeping arrangements were not as bad as I had imagined. I was to sleep on a "put-u-up" bed in Geon's room. We said our goodnights at just after one o'clock, with Joji promising to wake me at 4.15am. "Sleep well," he said as he closed the door.

"Geon came in a few minutes later with a towel for me." Hope you don't mind sharing a room, James. Who are you writing to?" he asked, seeing me tapping away on the iPad.

"I forgot to write to Jayne, my girlfriend, and mother, of course, saying I arrived OK," concentrating on my typing in the dim light of the side lamp.

"What is your girlfriend like, James?" Geon asked with interest.

I sent the e-mails and opened up my photo file. "This is her," I said proudly, showing him an image I had taken on our recent visit to Paris.

"She is very pretty. Are you going to marry her?"

"Good question, Geon. Very possibly. But I have not asked her yet."

Geon frowned. "Mayz will be disappointed, I think," he said quietly.

"I think she will find someone when she wants to." I offered, hoping her brother was not match-making on her behalf.

I fell asleep listening to Geon talking about his studies at Law school and was awoken by a gentle shake of the shoulder. "Come James, let's see the sunrise." Joji was standing over me. "You can sleep in the car for a while."

He had already gathered a bag with some breakfast and a flask as I stumbled out of the front door, trying to remember which shoes were mine from the dozens of pairs on the porch. We drove east, along the state highway, which was fairly free of traffic, except for the odd stray cow and early morning cyclists going to work.

However, by the time we reached our halfway point, near Thrikkariyoor, the traffic had built up considerably. Cars, vans, and more cyclists claimed every inch of the road as we continued on our journey. "Everyone likes to make an early start before it gets too hot," Joji explained, accounting for the extra traffic.

After a while, we turned off the highway, north to the Sholayar Reserve, at which point the traffic became considerably lighter.

We drove mainly in silence, and I did sleep for a few minutes here and there, but as the road became "off-road" there was no way I was going to sleep.

"Wouldn't a Land Rover be better for these roads?" I asked, partly joking.

Joji smiled back. "Relax. This old Honda is capable of good things." I was not convinced, as he slid the gear into second, climbing even higher. "I would have liked to have taken you to Kolukkumalai, up in the tea plantations, over 7,000ft above sea level. The views are wonderful, but maybe another time. Here we will be only 5,000ft high, but it is still a good view."

We climbed slowly for another thirty minutes along a dry hard road snaking its way up to our destination. The road was flanked each side by tall evergreens, and I glimpsed between the firs to see the flicker of streetlights way down below in the valley we had left behind.

We came to a purpose-built viewing lay-by arriving at a few minutes past six a.m.

"Just in time James, only a few more minutes. Did you have a camera?"

"No," I answered, trying to remember what I had brought with me. Nothing was the answer, not even my phone or iPad.

"Then you will have to rely on your memory, James. It's the one thing that won't get lost or erased. You will remember this morning forever," he said, guiding me closer to the spectator railings overlooking the sheer drop to the valley below and the lake beyond it. To the left of me was a cascade of mountains appearing one by one through the early morning mist. To my right, a high mountain climbed beyond the canopy of mist and clouds surrounding it. Then I saw the first glimpse of the sun's rays breaking through the horizon, dividing the blue of the lake with the bleakness of the night sky. Standing, spellbound, we witnessed what occurs every day of the year, without exception, but when witnessing for the very first time, it is like witnessing the birth of creation. Within seconds the sun became brighter and brighter, climbing before my eyes, transforming the sky from warm azure to shimmering indigo in seconds.

We stood transfixed for several more minutes, not realizing we had been joined by several other tourists and keen photographers who had set up tripods and expensive cameras to capture the moment. But Joji was right, there was no need for cameras - the memory of this morning will live with me forever. I just wish Jayne had been here.

We drove back down the other side of the mountain along the edge of a vast tea plantation. It looked like a giant mosaic maze stretching as far as the eye can see. After reaching the edge of the reserve we stopped again to have some tea, which was most welcome. The temperature can drop several degrees in the mountains so the warm chai was very welcoming. "So, James, was it worth only a few hours' sleep?" Joji asked, looking pleased.

"Of course. It was amazing. I have seen sunsets and sunrises before, but not in such a spectacular setting as this. Thank you. It is very much appreciated."

"Next time you visit we will go to the highest place in India, then you will see an even more spectacular sight, and I will take you on the tourist trail, and all the high spots in Cochin."

"I would like that. I am sorry I cannot stay longer, but I feel I do want to come back soon, hopefully with my girlfriend, Jayne."

Joji listened to me talk about Jayne and how we met, and how valuable she has been in this quest of mine. I talked about mother and my work, and my thoughts for the future. He listened with interest, nodding and smiling as always. "Joji, can I ask you something?"

"Of course, James, what is it?"

I hesitated a few seconds, not sure if this was the right thing to do, but I may not be given another chance, so I aired my thoughts. "Do you know anything about the circumstances of my Grandparents coming to England? I mean, the family was not Muslim, so why did they feel they had to leave when their relatives stayed on, here in Kerala."

Joji listened and looked on, puzzled, as if he had never considered the question before.

"I don't know, James. It is never spoken of, well not to me anyway, and certainly not between the family.

You can ask Gini if you think she knows, but it may stir up some bad memories. I do know one thing - she has not spoken to her sister since. You may not remember, but Jamilah did not come over for my wedding with your parents. She claimed to be ill, but I am not sure now."

"What are you saying, Joji? My Grandparents leaving India may not have been because of Partition?"

Chapter Sixteen

Jonathan met with Samuels at the Greyhound in Wimbledon. "Not to your liking, Johnny?"

"Not my usual taste in beer, but I am not here for that, am I?" Jonathan replied, sarcastically.

Samuels opened a shoulder bag and took out an A4 manila envelope and pushed it across the table. "This cost me a lot, so I want extra. I had to grease a few palms if you get my meaning."

Jonathan strummed the envelope several times, whilst sipping the obnoxious excuse for beer. "Firstly, I doubt you paid anyone, you are far too tight for that, and I know this file was a "closed" file. Why do you think I asked you? I know you still have contacts in the force. I was sure you knew someone who owes you a favor or two, and it seems I was right," he said matter-of-factly.

"Smug bastard. I have read that and it says only one person was under suspicion, some young lawyer, with a very influential Judge for a father. I wonder who put pressure on the CPS to bury it." Samuels spat out the rhetorical question, knowing he had touched a nerve.

If Jonathan was caught off guard, he did not show it. He kept his cool. "Here's what we agreed, two hundred. Don't spend it all at once." And picked up the envelope before heading for the door, and out of the rat-hole excuse for a pub.

. . .

On Sunday everyone went to church. "Are you coming with us, James? You do go to church don't you?" Mayz asked.

"Leave James alone, Mayz." Aunt Gini called over, adjusting her best Sunday sari. In fact, all the ladies looked stunning in the most colorful saris I had seen. "You ladies look wonderful. I must find time to buy one for Jayne. I have been promising her one for a long time."

"No problem," Joji said, "we can go shopping this afternoon, after lunch, in Fort Cochin. You will like it there, very touristy. Now, are you coming to church? You will find it ... different ... trust me. I was right about yesterday, wasn't I?"

"How can I refuse, but let me change first." I unpacked my selection of kurtas and dhotis and selected the most appropriate for church. The orange kurta shirt with gilt trim was straightforward to wear, but I had no idea how to tie a dhoti. I called down from the bedroom. "Hi, Geon, Joji, anyone. Can you help me a minute."

The door open and Mayz stood there laughing at my predicament. "Everyone is in the car waiting for you. Have you never tied a dhoti before James?"

"Obviously not, but I think uncle Joji should . . ."

"Nonsense, come here," and Mayz pulled me closer and took the length of material from behind me, standing very close now, faces almost touching, and wound the cloth around my waist, folding it once to make a pleat. "Now, stand still James, this is the tricky part." She took one corner of the cloth and tied it onto a knot. "Now pull tight James, and tuck this into your pants, if you are wearing any that is."

I grabbed the knotted cloth and stepped back a pace. "Thank you, Mayz. Go tell them I will be down in a moment."

She gave me a sullen look and leant forward to kiss me on the cheek, before leaving the room.

I quickly pressed the knotted material into my pants and hoped that was enough to hide my modesty.

"You look great," Joji remarked as I climbed into the now packed car. "I didn't know you had a dhoti with you."

"It's a long story," I said, not wanting to relate the whole shopping saga.

"Yes, you do look good James. I hope it holds up OK." Mayz giggled, along with a laugh from Geon and Rayyan.

I had grown up neither a Hindu, Muslim nor Christian. I had not given any thought to why my parents had not adopted a belief, especially as my Grandparents had apparently fled religious turmoil back in India. They had adopted a liberal stance when bringing up their own daughter, my mother, and she, in turn, allowed me to choose my own path. My father was also not religious to any extent, so I grew up at a distance from any church education or practical participation.

I had however over the years attended two weddings, one Christian and one Muslim. One Christian funeral, a baptism and a bar mitzvah, so I felt I knew roughly how a service was conducted, and what to expect in the way of hymns and incantations.

How wrong could I have been? The church was St Peters and St Paul's Basilica, a large white-walled building built by the Portuguese back in 1678. The wooden vaulted roof stretched at least one hundred feet, and the church was packed to capacity, so much so, loudspeakers had been set up outside for the overspill congregation.

"Keep close, James," Joji called out. "There are seats half-way down the nave on right. Our friends are holding them for us. Maybe a little tight fit today."

We found two rows of bench seats. The men sat on one bench and the women behind us. Mayz was directly behind me and I could feel her breath on my neck every time she spoke. I looked around in awe of the magnificence of the interior. A row of wide, high windows stretched along each side of the church walls, giving ample natural light to the interior.

Thirty or more rows of wooden pews spanned each side of the Nave, and there was standing room only in both aisles and most of the nave. Soon music filled the church - music I had never heard in a church before. Not solemn or even remotely sacred, but joyous and harmonious. There must have been a choir somewhere; unfortunately my sight was obscured by a tall white pillar, but the sound was unmistakable. And when the whole congregation joined in it was just heavenly. I can't say I was instantly converted, but it did make me think what a pleasure it was to attend such a service and witness the joy these followers were getting from their faith.

Outside in the heat of the midday sun, we mixed with friends and watched children play on the grass. I was introduced to dozens of people, all nodding and smiling, pleased to meet and greet a relative from England, and wanting to know why I was alone, where was my wife, what I did for a living, how old was I … the questions were not meant to be intrusive, just genuinely inquisitive. Many spoke in local dialectic but Joji was translating, and I just nodded and smiled until it was time to go. "Well, James, what do you think of our little church?" Joji asked, walking arm-in-arm with his mother back to the car.

"It was wonderful. I have never experienced anything like that before." And I don't know why, but added, "I can't imagine why Grandfather and Grandmother would have wanted to leave all this behind."

Aunty Gini stopped walking, and I thought she was going to faint. "I am OK," she said tersely, "it's the heat." Joji ushered her into the car as quickly as possible and turned on the air conditioning. Aunt Gini glanced at me through the car window with an expression that could be only described as deathly. What had I said to make her react that way? I only had a few hours left to find out.

Back at the house, I checked my emails. One from Jayne - very personal. One from mother – very predictable, sending usual messages etc. to everyone, but still nothing from Jonathan. I was about to Skype him but realized it was only 6.00am back home . . . that wouldn't be fair, would it? I sent an email instead, asking if he had any news from Samuels, and to Skype me as soon as he could.

. . .

Back home Jonathan read the opening paragraph to the crime report, twice:

"Deceased: Ms Pamela Norton, resident of Melbourne, Australia. Died on or around 12th September 1965. No connection to the "Nude Murders".

"Bloody hellfire, James. What have you opened up?"

Chapter Seventeen

Monday morning was spent racing around buying presents for everyone. It was hard to know what to get each of them, but I felt it was necessary, and I wanted to leave a "thank you" for putting me up at short notice.   Joji especially deserved something. He had been driving me everywhere and had not worked for two days because of my visit. My flight back to New Delhi was at 2.45pm so I only had a couple of hours to do some shopping, get back, pack and say my goodbyes to those who were left. Gigitta, George and Rayyan had gone back home Sunday afternoon, and Geon had to leave early for college, so we had said goodbye at breakfast. That left Mayz, who said she had a morning free so could go shopping with me, if I needed some company. As it turned out she was very helpful in choosing gifts for each of her relatives, and of course herself. She also helped me buy a sari for Jayne and mother.

Back at the house, we unpacked our shopping in my bedroom, and I quickly wrote names on each of the gifts. "Here, Mayz, this is for you. I hope you like it." I said laughing and handed her the silver bracelet she had chosen for herself. "It is very nice, thank you, James," she said with a mischievous smile, and came nearer to kiss me on the cheek, or so I thought. She clasped her hands to my face and kissed me fully on the lips. I was so taken aback, I could not move for a few seconds, which seemed like minutes. "Mayz." I eventually spluttered. "You cannot do that. We are related, for one, and I have someone back home. Please don't be offended. You are a lovely lady and I am sure there are many young men who would . . . err . . . love to go out with you." By now I was well and truly tongue-tied. She looked hurt at first, and then smiled. "Oh, James, we are not so close blood tied, and I will make you very happy," and continued to hug me and kiss my neck. Then I felt her right-hand slide down my back which ended up clutching my bottom.

"Please stop, Mayz." I have to get ready. My flight is in a couple of hours. Just then the bedroom door opened and Auntie Gini shuffled in. "Aunty, shouldn't you be resting. Where is Uncle Jogin?"

Aunt Gini waved a defiant arm in the air. "I am fine, stop fussing. You sound like my son." Then proceeded to talk to Mayz in their own language, and from what I could make out from expressions and gestures, was not a polite conversation. Mayz turned to me and shrugged, then blew me kiss behind her Grandmother's back as she slipped out of the room without a care in the world.

"She means no harm, Auntie, she . . ." but Gini held up a hand. "She is foolish. She should have married by now, but I will not have her flirting with any of her relations."

Aunt Gini stepped closer to the end of the bed and sat down. "I wanted to talk to you. You deserve to know the truth," she said, looking away from me.

"What are you talking about? What truth?" I asked, wondering if I should call Joji or Uncle Jogin. She grabbed my arm. "You asked about my sister, and why she and her husband fled to England."

"Yes," I said, hesitantly. "But it's not . . ."

"Listen," she interrupted, "my sister had an affair with Jogin and became pregnant with your mother."

I sat on the bed, mouth open, unable to utter a sound, trying to understand what she had just said. It didn't make sense at first, but the more I thought about it, the clearer it became. There was no religious division between the families. Grandmother wanted to leave because she was pregnant with mother, and told the Partition story to support their leaving.

"How do you know this Auntie? Did she tell you?"

"No. She did not have to. My sister married young and had no experience with men. She had been married a month and had still not . . . consummated their marriage," she looked down as if ashamed.

"Auntie, you do not have to tell me this . . ."

"But I do, James. I must pass this secret to you before I leave this body."

"Don't say that, you . . ." but she pressed a finger to my lips.

"Let me finish my boy, and then we will never speak of this again." I nodded, reluctantly, as part of me wanted to know the truth as well.

"One day I found bloodstains on our bed. I quickly washed the sheets and said nothing at first. Then, when Jamilah said she was pregnant, I told her I knew. She was horrified and said she had brought shame on the family and wanted to kill herself. I persuaded her she was young and had her whole life ahead of her. It was I who suggested they leave for England under the threat of Partition."

"But uncle Sami, what did he believe? Why would he agree?" I asked, now gripped by this story.

Aunt Gini smiled once again. "That was easy. Back then Sami's family were Muslim and I persuaded them to escape what may be a terrible conflict - either staying here in Kerala or making Jamilah go to the north, to a divided country. They chose England."

I stood up and looked out to the street below. I watched people going about their daily lives, doing what they do every day. How many of them are carrying around secrets I wondered.

"James, are you OK? Please tell me you will not say anything to anyone, especially your mother."

Aunt Gini stood, and I held her fragile hands and kissed her cheek. "I promise," I whispered, and she smiled again before leaving me to finish packing. But I sat on the bed again going over what I had been told. How many other secrets am I to be entrusted with? First Michael Parker with his long lost lover, now Grandmother having an affair . . . what else could possibly top that?

I was brought out of my trance by the iPad lighting up and the familiar Skype jingle announcing an incoming call. It was Jonathan. "Hi, James. How's the weather, bloody cold here."

"Good to see you too, Jonathan. Make it quick. I have to leave for the airport soon."

"OK then. Here goes. Samuels came through. I have the case file. Are you ready for this?"

"Come on man, it can't be any worse than what I have . . . never mind . . . just tell me."

"OK. Pamela Norton may have been murdered, it's inconclusive, and that's why it was probably a sealed case . . . James, are you there, I can't see you anymore, just a ceiling fan."

I had let the iPad slip out of my hands onto the bed. I stared at the window for some time before it dawned on me what Jonathan had just said; my previous assumptions were right, either Martin Sterne or Michael Parker could be a murderer.

"James, James . . . are you there? Can you hear me?"

"Sorry, just getting over the shock. Are you sure about this?"

"Just saying what was in the report, James."

"Can you scan it and email it to me? I can read it on the flight back. Don't do anything or say anything to anyone, is that clear?"

"Clear, James, one hundred per cent. I will email this over soon. Have a good flight. Over and out." And the screen went blank, as did my mind for a while.

'*Top that*' I had said a short while ago, and he certainly had.

Chapter Eighteen

Joji dropped me at the airport just in time to check-in. "So, it was a flying visit, James, but I hope you will not forget us, and come back one day, yes," Joji said smiling as we hugged, which seemed quite natural.

"Thank you for everything, Joji. You have been great. I am sorry it was short notice, and a short stay, but I am glad I have met you all. Mother and Grandmother will be very pleased."

"Write soon, and love to everyone in England, James." And he was gone.

I slept some of the flight back to New Delhi as Jonathan had not emailed me the police report he had promised, but I was restless. I kept thinking about what Aunt Gini had told me. It seemed like a dream - a bad dream. Why me, I kept asking myself, looking out of the aircraft window at the fading light. Michael Parker's secret, Grandmother's secret, and now Sterne and Parker's involvement in a possible murder - I was not sure I could handle the burden of it all. I wished Jayne was with me. I needed to hold and hug someone I loved right now. I eventually reached my hotel around eleven, and immediately checked my emails again. Only one from Jayne, but that was all I wanted. It was not too late to Skype her, so I did. I touched the screen as soon as she answered. "Hi, love, hope you can talk."

"Yes, of course. Just thinking of leaving work anyway. How was the trip?"

"Bit of a roller-coaster. We did so much in a couple of days, Uncle Joji was great, took me everywhere. They want us to visit again soon."

"Glad all went well, James. Did your mother get in touch? Your Granddad is not too well."

"Hell no, she hasn't texted me about that. Where is he?"

"He is at home, and the doctor said he may have to go into hospital for a few days observation. But I get the impression it's just old age, James."

"I will visit as soon as I get back. I need to talk to mother anyway . . ." but stopped short for fear of saying too much.

"Are you OK, you look tired. When is your flight back?"

"I'm fine. I just want to get this over with now love, and spend some time with you," I said touching the screen, adding, "Love you lots."

"Love you too. Have you heard from Jonathan? He's gone very quiet lately."

I bit my lip, which was a silly thing to do on a video call. "Yes, he said something about following up a lead on Pamela's death."

"James, you didn't tell me that. What lead? I thought she died from an overdose or something"

"Yes, well . . . we may have another angle on that. Look, I promise to fill you in when I have all the facts. It's just supposition for now and . . ."

"James Lacey, don't use legal jargon on me. After all we have been through I would expect you to keep me up-to-date."

"Sorry love, but I really don't have all the facts, and that's the truth. I am waiting for Porky to email me some reports, and I will let you know the outcome as soon as I have them, I promise. Now I have to get some sleep. I will call you when I land on Wednesday."

"OK," she said, still looking hurt, "I hope you have brought me a very expensive present to make up for it James."

. . .

I must have had some kind of jet-lag as I slept in until ten o'clock the next morning. I was awoken, for the second time, by the maid hammering on the bedroom door, then letting herself in. "Sorry," she said, and left immediately.

I wondered if I should call the Professor to make sure he was there today. What if he only worked part-time? What if Mr Sharma had warned him I was asking for him and frightened him away? Too many *"what if's"*. I reached the ASI offices at 11.15am, which now felt very familiar with its garden walkway and modern glass entrance hall and air-conditioned reception.

Ms Singh was still there, at her sentry post. "Mr Lacey, hello. I was not expecting you back . . . I mean didn't Prof . . . I mean Mr . . ." And she suddenly stopped talking and ran out of the reception.

I could have followed her as on my last visit, but this time decided to sit and wait. Surprisingly, after a few minutes, she returned. "Please come this way, Mr Lacey," and indicated to follow her along the same corridor I had seen before.

I felt a surge of relief coupled with anxiety when she showed me the Professor's office, the same one he shares with Mr Sharma. However, my heart dropped when she opened the door and I saw only Mr Sharma sitting there.

Ms Singh turned to me and smiled, and nodded towards Mr Sharma. "The Prof . . . Mr Lacey." and she left, leaving me somewhat bewildered.

"Mr Sharma, I was given to understand that Professor Siddique-Chaudhary would be here today. You told me . . ."

"He is here young man. You are talking to him."

I stared at the man sitting behind the desk, then I saw the nameplate on the desk; Professor Siddiqui-Chaudhary.

"I am sorry, Mr Lacey, I do owe you an explanation and an apology. Please take a seat." He said, gesturing me to sit down.

"I don't understand. Why the charade? You could have saved me a lot of time Professor." If I sounded cross, I probably was. This elderly grey-haired man sitting opposite me was smiling as if everything was normal. Why does everyone have to bloody smile?

"You stage-managed all this is didn't you? Fooling me to believe you were someone else - persuading me to go to Kerala . . . ."

"Yes, and how was that James? You did say you had not seen your relatives since you were very young."

"That's not the point," I said, raising my voice and sitting forward. "I could have been home by now, with my girlfriend."

He nodded and smiled. "Yes, of course. But tell me, was the visit to Kerala rewarding?"

"Rewarding? What do you mean? I met my Grandparent's relatives and cousins, and yes, they were nice people, and I . . ." I leant back in the chair, "yes, OK, it was a very interesting trip, and I did learn more about them than I knew, so thank you for that, but why the deceit Professor?"

He opened the desk drawer and took out a framed photograph, and looked at it affectionately.

"I did indeed work with Lady Grey, sorry, Dianne Holland, for many years.

She was a wonderful lady, and a dear friend," he said, looking with fondness at whoever he was looking at.

"Lady Grey?" I asked. "I have not heard that name before."

The Professor smiled. "It was an affectionate nickname she was given because of her love of Earl Grey tea."

Of course. This fitted in with what Louis had told us in Paris, and his thoughtful gift of a tea-caddy.

"James, I know you want answers." The Professor said, bringing me back to reality. He passed me the photo he had been holding. "This is her on her wedding day, in 1992. She married the Spanish *chargé d' affaires*, at the Spanish Embassy here in New Delhi."

I studied the photo. There were about seven or eight guests, other than the bride and groom all looking very smart. Dianne was, however, radiant. She was looking slightly sideways at her husband, not straight ahead, and I could tell she was in love.

I identified the Professor, but no one else.

"She looks wonderful," I said, almost reverently. "Is she alive, Professor?" I added, looking him in the eye.

His face changed, and I knew I had his attention. "You wanted me out of the way for a reason. Was it to call her and warn her I was asking about her? I am not a bad guy. It's to her advantage I find her, Professor." I had to throw a line, and hope he would bite.

I handed him back the photo and he looked at it again before replacing it in the desk drawer. "Yes . . . she is alive," he said slowly, considering each word carefully now.

My heart was pounding . . . positive proof . . . at last. But where was she? "And?" I asked, expectantly.

"That is all you can know, Mr Lacey. She does not want any inheritance," he replied seriously.

"But Professor . . ." I hesitated . . . "It is more complicated than that. I have been searching for months and travelled far and wide to find her. You tell me she is alive, and then cut me off without any explanation."

I was almost begging, and why not. I felt cheated and annoyed. I had been manipulated all along and was now about to be turned out with hardly anything that justified a seven thousand mile trip.

"I am truly sorry young man. I cannot help you any further. I have said too much already. I must ask you to please now leave, without causing a fuss." He then rose and came around to open the door for me.

I sighed, and realized I was shaking my head, and let out a muted laugh.

"What is funny?" the Professor asked.

"Nothing . . . nothing at all Professor. Thank you for your time, but if you are in touch with her please persuade her to contact me. It really is important." I appealed one more time.

I walked back towards the now familiar reception, and into the blinding sunlight, which seemed all too appropriate.

. . .

Back at the hotel, I called the airline to see if I could change my flight for one that evening, but the best they could offer was one the next morning, via Dubai. At least I would not have to sit around for ten hours doing nothing, except getting more and more annoyed and frustrated.

It was too early to call Jayne, so I texted instead and told her of my new timetable. Jonathan had at last emailed the police and post-mortem reports, but I was not in the mood to read them now. I felt numb and deflated - slapped in the face for delving too deeply into someone else's affairs.

I lay on the bed and closed my eyes, hoping sleep would take me through to morning so I did not have to think about what to do next, or what answers to give Michael Parker. If I started questioning everything I have learnt on this journey I wouldn't sleep for a week.

Instead of sleeping, I laid on my back, staring at the ceiling. I blinked at the innocuous plain white canvas above me and saw faint shadows leaping here and there, gradually taking form. I blinked again but they were still there. I closed my eyes and prayed for sleep. I never pray, so I was not answered. I was not susceptible to fantasizing but felt I was looking at a scene I had not visited for many years. The brow of a hill took shape with woodland surrounding it, with a stream winding its way through fir trees until reaching a silent pool. "My God." I called out, "Merlin . . . is that you."

When I was young my father would read to me every evening. Children's books and poems mainly. Books I could use my imagination to work with; Grimm's Fairytales, Hans Christian Andersen, Dr Seuss and many others.

On my eighth birthday he gave me a book by Thomas Barron called *The Seven Songs of Merlin.*

It was not an old book by any means, on the contrary, but the subject matter was a re-telling of an old legend. The young Merlin had to save his mother by finding an elixir - undertaking a hazardous and perilous journey to unseen lands. Merlin had to master each of the seven songs to give him the strength he needed to succeed. Each song had a soul name, but I couldn't remember them all;

Changing - All of us, all living things, have the potential to change
Protecting - The best way to protect something is to set it free
Leaping - Everything is connected to everything else
Binding - The strongest bonds are of the heart

Perhaps these were all I needed to remember, especially; *Everything is connected to everything else.*

When I looked at the ceiling again it was just a plain white ceiling. I got up and opened the heavy blackout curtains to find it was now nearing sunrise. Had I slept all that time? Had I dreamed it all? Even if I had, Dad had been the catalyst and he had reminded me of the parallel between me and Merlin - our quest - 'Thanks, Dad' I whispered. "I know what I must do now."

I wanted to give up a few weeks ago, but Jayne made me see that I had to finish it. Now, Dad has shown me I still have a job to do. *Everything is connected to everything else.*

Chapter Nineteen

On the flight to Dubai, I opened my iPad and read the police and post-mortem reports Jonathan had sent me.

Sometime between 6th September and 8th September 1965, Miss Pamela Norton was discovered by her landlord, Duncan Bishop, dead in her flat. Police were called to the scene on 9th September at 10.33am and discovered Miss Norton's body on the floor of the sitting-room. The body was clothed. (no connection to the Nude Murders was identified)

There were no signs of a break-in or disturbance, and as far as the officers could see, nothing has been taken. Evidence showed Ms Norton had been smoking marijuana, and had consumed a lot of alcohol, which the attached post-mortem report concurs with. There were also several non-prescription antidepressant drugs found near her body, although the post-mortem could not find any evidence of these being taken.

Initial conclusion was suicide or accidental death.

However, further evidence gathered showed Ms Norton had been visited a number of times by an ex. resident of the premises, Mr Martin Sterne. Witness statements confirm he had visited Ms Norton two or three days prior to her body being discovered, and one neighbor heard loud shouting coming from the premises. In his statement, Mr Sterne recalls visiting the premises to collect post and had a run-in with Miss Norton who 'seemed under the influence' of alcohol.

A recent resident, Miss Dianne Holland has not been traced. Her boyfriend of several months, Mr Michael Parker, was interviewed and confirmed Miss Holland left suddenly five weeks prior to Miss Norton's death.

Both Mr Sterne and Mr Parker had possible motive and access to the premises.

Mr Sterne has accused Mr Parker of jealousy, claiming Miss Norton kept a letter she was to give him from Miss Holland, concerning her disappearance. Mr Sterne claims there was a heated discussion between these two persons and they parted on bad terms.

Mr Parker in his statement claims Mr Sterne despised Miss Norton and was a racist.

A second post-mortem examination was carried out on the 21st September, which proved inconclusive as to the cause of death.

I then read the two post-mortem reports, which were almost identical in their conclusions, that traces of marijuana and alcohol were high in the blood and urine. No other drugs were traced, and she had not eaten prior to her death for at least six hours.

The post-mortem examiner concluded accidental death while under the influence.

Another report from the Coroner agreed with these findings and assumed the case was closed. If that was so, why was the report "sealed"?

All very circumstantial, as DCI Osborne had concluded, so why did he think there was more to investigate. I recalled what Mr Wilkes had related to me about finding a letter he thought had been written to Martin Sterne . . . how did that letter turn up in Sterne's room? Perhaps DCI Osborne was more intuitive than he realized.   I also wondered if he was still alive.

. . .

I emailed Jonathan with what I had found out from my meeting with the Professor and asked him to start searching for whoever the Spanish *charge d' affaires* was in Delhi in 1992. And check out DCI Osborne.

Jayne collected me from the airport and I was so glad to see her. I dropped my case and hugged her, never wanting to let her go. "I am sorry my love. I promise never to leave you again." And we stood there in each other's arms for a while longer.

"Come on, let's get you home . . . and to bed," she said, kissing me again.

. . .

Professor "Rafi" Siddique-Chaudhary wrote again to Lady Grey;

My dear friend, the problem person has now left me alone, and all is back to normal.

I look forward very much to seeing you and your husband next year at the Anniversary Convention.

Yours, Rafi

. . .

Thursday was a blur, and I did not feel like confronting Morris or Michael Parker the next day either, so I took a "sickie", as did Jayne. We laid in bed Friday morning listening to the world go by but finding the strength to make toast and coffee, which in turn give me strength to make love to my love - several times. "You must take a "sickie" more often, James Lacey," Jayne said, snuggling up to me, face to face. She saw my thoughtful expression. "Hey, no thinking about "you know who" today. It's no thinking day, James."

I smiled and kissed her nose. "Of course, but it's not possible to go through the waking day and not to think about . . ."

"James Lacey, you are seriously close to a tickling marathon." And she started to move her hands in line with my waist. The only defense I could think of was to move on top of her and pin her arms to the pillow.

"James, that's not fair," she exclaimed, meekly. Soon she had forgotten about attacking me, and I had certainly forgotten about. . ?

. . .

Over breakfast Saturday morning I did have to come back to reality and face up to my responsibilities. "I think we need to hold a summit," I suggested. "You, me and Jonathan, to decide how we proceed, so I can write my final report."

I filled Jayne in with the police and post-mortem reports and all that had happen in India, with the exception of my Aunt's mind-blowing revelations. I felt bad not confiding in her after all we had been through, but it had to remain a secret; one I wish I could forget.

Jonathan came over for Sunday lunch, and I was pleased to see him more than I would ever admit. "So, where's my present you bloody globe-trotter." He moaned, in a not very convincing Welsh accent. (Considering the line of work he is in, he has never been able to prove his Welsh ancestry satisfactorily).

"Lovely to see you too," I said, after our manly hug. "I did find an interesting CD at the airport. It's a rather good band from Bangalore, Righu Dixit. In fact, I may even keep it."

"You tight . . ."

"Hey, boys, stop it, or no lunch," Jayne said, waving a wooden spoon at the pair of us.

"Hope he bought you something sexy, my angel. Leaving you all alone like that."

"Stop making mischief, Johnny, and yes he did as a matter of fact. A very fetching sari and . . . what is it, James . . . a dressing gown or housecoat?"

"Sounds like an excuse for a fashion parade later," Jonathan said, relishing the prospect.

"We have a lot to discuss, so nothing is going to side-track you. We need clear heads today." I said, sounding serious enough to stop the conversation for a while.

Lunch was subdued as we each went over the events of the past six months. Jayne and I ate half-heartedly while Jonathan devoured everything, and had seconds. "I am glad you still have a good appetite, Jonathan," I said, pouring a glass of non-alcoholic wine.

"No wonder you have lost your appetite, man, drinking that diluted excuse for wine."

"I need a clear head, as I said earlier, and I think we should talk about where we are now."

Jayne looked at me and smiled, touching my hand. Jonathan was about to satirize the moment and hold my other hand, but luckily changed his mind.

"OK," I started, taking a deep breath, "do we all understand where we are at?" Jayne and Jonathan remained silent, preferring to let me do the summarizing. "OK then, as I see it we have discovered the following;

Dianne Greenway/Holland left Michael Parker in August 1965 and had his child, a daughter called Kimberly.

Dianne took Kimberly with her to Paris in 1969

She then worked in several countries including Egypt, Pakistan, Korea and India.

She married in 1992 to a Spanish gentleman from the Spanish Embassy. Probably honeymooned in Greece. Are you with me so far?"

"Absolutely," Jonathan confirmed, pouring another glass of wine.

"Yes love, carry on," Jayne said, reassuringly.

"I know Jonathan has something to add which I hope is of interest, but I want to go over the "other" aspects that have arisen during our investigations." I sipped some faux-wine.

"The revelation of Pamela Norton's death has become a complication. We have to decide if Michael Parker or Martin Sterne were reasonable for her death, or if it was an accident, or even suicide."

"But James, surely the police investigation came to the conclusion she died accidentally – a mixture of booze and drugs." Jayne said.

"Yes, I agree, but DCI Osborne, the investigating officer, had reservations. Johnny, did you manage to track him?"

"Yes, and unfortunately he died in 1994, so a dead end there," he said, smirking at his own joke.

I sighed but refrained from encouraging him further. Jayne shot a look that told him to "grow-up".

"So, do we take this further?"

"What! Exhume her, and no I am not joking before you start on me." Jonathan shot in.

I looked ahead in thought. "You are not seriously considering that, James. It's not right." Jayne agreed.

"Perhaps not, but it would be good to have proof-positive, somehow," I said, feeling decidedly weary of where this was going.

"May I say something that may have a bearing on your decision, James?" Jonathan said, soberly.

"Of course my friend, what do have?"

"Well, I managed to find a Senora D Valera. Alfonso Valera was the charge d' affaires at that time in Delhi. They now reside near Madrid. It's too good a match to ignore."

I should have felt elated, but something in me triggered a note of caution – it could be another false hope.

"James . . . are you Ok? Did you hear what Johnny just said? It sounds your professor helped after all." Jayne said, squeezing my hand.

Jonathan nodded. "Yes, the name and location look good. It has to be worth considering."

Of course it was. Could I go to Michael Parker knowing I had not pursued all the leads? Well, I could of course, but Merlin's voice in my head sang out: *The best way to protect something is to set it free* – perhaps Dianne Holland does need to be set free from her deep secret. Perhaps the only way to free her is to let her tell her story.

"Jayne, love. You remember when I said I would never leave you again."

Chapter Twenty

The door opened slowly. A young girl in her early teens looked at me curiously, and stood with the door only slightly ajar, ready to close it again quickly.

"Si, Senor" she whispered.

I heard a voice in the background calling to her in Spanish "Lucie, who is there darling?"

The voice was an older woman's voice. Clear and distinctive. I was hard put to tell the nationality, although the accent seemed Spanish.

"I do not know Grandma," the girl replied in Spanish, still in a whisper.

My Spanish was not conversational, just enough to order beer and tapas, so I plumped for English and smiled. "Hola, I am looking for Dianne Valera, or maybe Dianne Greenway."

I stared at the girl who did not move or respond. I was about to repeat the question, this time in some broken Spanish when I heard the other woman's voice coming from behind the girl, but closer to her this time, although I still could not see her.

"Who is asking for Dianne Greenway?" the question was in English and took me by surprise.

I hesitated a few seconds before gaining my concentration. "Madam, err Senora, I have been looking for Dianne Greenway on the instructions of my client."

There was a silence for what seemed like forever. The next question came more measured and inquisitively. "Who is your client, and why would this person know Dianne Greenway?"

I thought quickly. I needed to see this woman. I had a feeling, after all this time I was finally at journey's end. My heart was pounding fast.

"Madam, my client is dying, and as for why I am here, I can only reveal that to the lady in question." I ground my teeth hoping I had said enough to gain entrance.

A hand appeared on the young girl's shoulder, and a woman slowly appeared out of the shadows of the shaded hallway. To my relief, she was smiling a gentle, reassuring smile, and I somehow knew as soon as I saw her, and before she spoke the words I had so longed to hear, I had found Dianne Greenway.

"You had better come in, young man. I am Dianne Valera, once Dianne Greenway, and tell me who is dying."

I entered through the grand double doors into a large reception hall. Dianne was standing at the bottom of the stairs, next to a small occasional table housing a large blue and white ceramic bowl. In the opposite corner stood an attractive tall white umbrella stand, decorated with giant red English roses and green foliage.

"Thank you for seeing me. My name is James ..." I hesitated.

Have you forgotten your name?" she asked smiling.

"No, sorry . . . it's a long story. My name is James Lacey."

She stepped forward and we shook hands. "This is Lucie," she said, and I nodded to the young woman standing next to me. Now, standing closer to the girl, I could see a faint resemblance to someone I had seen in a photograph.

"Come into the lounge. Would you like tea? You look as if you could do with some refreshment."

"Thank you, that would be good. I have been walking around in the heat looking for the house."

We went into a spectacularly large reception room. The tall vaulted ceiling was decorated with finely painted watercolors, depicting iconic ancient buildings from around the world.

The south wall had tall, almost floor to ceiling windows facing the front of the house, and from the north side, large French style double doors provided entrance to an equally large conservatory.

"Please, James, take a seat," and she turned to Lucie and spoke in English. "Please ask Maria to bring tea, my dear."

I wandered the room taking in the splendor of the decor and the artefacts that were on show. Although there seemed to be many objects, paintings, books and furniture in the room, the room did not feel overly cluttered. It had a distinctly warm and inviting quality about it. It wanted you to discover its secrets, and admire them.

Dianne saw I was captivated by the room. "So, James . . . can I call you James, or do you have another name?" she smiled again, and I realized she was teasing me.

"Yes, of course. Sorry about earlier. I will explain if we have time, maybe later." I replied.

My eye had caught a most beautiful white round vase encased in a glass display.

"I see you are admiring my Moon Jar. It was a gift from a very dear friend after working in Seoul. I was on a Sabbatical from Delhi."

"It is beautiful," I said, stating the obvious. Curiously, though, looking closer I noticed the shape was not perfectly symmetrical on one side, giving it a quality of individualism that would have been lost in a perfect shape. "Is it old?" I asked, not knowing anything about the subject.

"Around three to four hundred years. Originally from Korea, the Choson dynasty."

"Did you collect all of these items during your work as an archaeologist?" I asked.

Dianne looked a little surprised. "You seem to know a lot about me, James. I am intrigued now."

I turned to face her but she had walked over to the conservatory. "Come, let's sit out here, its cooler this time of day."

I was about to follow when I glanced once more at the Moon Jar and noticed a small hairline crack running from the lip downwards, for about four inches. "Shame it has a crack in it, but I suppose it's to be expected after all these years." Then, talking to myself I muttered, "That's how the light gets in."

Dianne froze, and turned towards me with a look of horror mixed with inquisitiveness. "What did you say just then?"

"Oh, just that it had a crack in it. I thought it . . "

"No, after that, James. You said something else," she was now standing next to me.

"Oh, just a line I heard once: *Everything has a crack in it, That's how the light gets in.*" And I noticed her mouthing the same words, almost hypnotically.

"Are you OK? Do you want me to get someone?" She had gone a little pale and I was afraid she was about to faint.

"No, no, I'm fine," she insisted, coming back to normality.

"Where did you hear that phrase, James? It comes from an old Leonard Cohen song."

"Well, yes . . . I think we need to sit down I will tell you the whole story. Then it will become clear."

We sat in the cool conservatory and I opened my briefcase and took out the now thick file, containing all the notes and information I had gathered over the past six months on Dianne Holland/Greenway.

I took a deep breath. "Dianne, my office was asked by one of our clients to try and find Dianne Holland. My client is Michael Parker."

If she was surprised she did not show any emotion. She smiled gently, and I saw for the first time how the years of working in extreme climates had aged her prematurely but was certainly still attractive, and I could see why so many men would have fallen for her.

"So you have not been looking for me in connection with my sister?"

"No, but I have met her. Dianne, have you heard she died last June. She died in her sleep, peacefully."

"No, I hadn't. I thought something had happened when Rafi told me. I know you have met him, James," she tipped her head down and closed her eyes momentarily.

"James, I must confess, Rafi emailed me and told me of your enquiries. I thought you were looking for me in connection with my sister because you mentioned an inheritance and assumed she had died."

"So you have known all along I was looking for you?" I said with a hint of firmness in my voice.

"James, please don't be angry. Dear Rafi was only looking out for me. He is probably the only other person in the world who knows my story. Not even my husband knows everything," she said with a heartfelt tone in her voice. I looked back up at her.

"Rafi became suspicious after your initial emails, then turning up in person - it threw him a little, that is why he talked you into going away for the weekend so he could contact me - I had no idea it was on behalf of

Michael Parker you wanted to see me. I told him to be discreet and send you away no matter what it was you wanted with me."

"Oh, he sent me away, twice in fact," I said without elaborating.

There was an awkward silence again for a while, and I was not sure if she wanted to carry on, but suddenly asked, "How did Sinead die?"

"In her sleep. She had a heart condition. We had been to visit her one afternoon, that is Jayne, my girlfriend, and I, and she was talking freely about when you were both young. She was a very nice lady, and we were very sad to hear she had died after we had just met her."

I could see Dianne was remembering again. "I was so unkind to her all those years back," and she closed her eyes in memory, but I could see no tears.

"She wanted you to have your share of your parents' estate if you want it. I can make all the arrangements."

"That's good of you, James, but no. I did not want it then and I don't need it now," she said, looking around the room, acknowledging she was obviously wealthy enough.

"But perhaps, if there is an estate to dispose of I will give you the details of a charitable fund that it can go to."

"Yes, of course. Leave it to me." I was glad of the chance to keep in touch with this intriguing lady.

"So, Michael Parker. That is a name I have not heard for a long time. Why did he want you to find me after so many years?"

"As I mentioned earlier, he is dying. Cancer I believe. His wife died a few years ago and he now feels he is running out of time. He wants to know why you left him all those years ago without leaving a note or an explanation. And if the rumors were true . . . that you were pregnant."

Just then a lady came in with a tray of tea. "Thank you, Maria. I will pour," she said in Spanish. Then she had an afterthought. "Maria, tell cook we have one more for lunch please." Alone again. "James you will stay for lunch. I think we have a lot to talk over."

"Thank you. That is kind," and I opened the folder on my lap. The Letter was there on top. The manila envelope was not as clean and pristine as it had been when it was given to me six months ago. After travelling halfway around the world, and escaping a couple of times, it was now decidedly . . . distressed - I think is the term Dianne would use in her line of work.

"My quest was to find you, and if so, give you this letter."

Dianne leant back on the sofa, thinking. "What is in it?" she eventually asked.

"I don't know. Questions I suspect," and placed it on the coffee table between us. She did not attempt to pick it up, just sat there staring at it.

"James. How much do you know?"

I looked up from the copperplate name on the envelope and it finally dawned on me I had actually achieved what Michael Parker had asked me to do. I blinked and focused again, Jayne and Jonathan will be pleased.

"Well, Michael Parker called me in one day and told me how he and you met in the London Museum in 1965, and eventually became lovers. He told me after six months you suddenly left without any word of explanation."

"You said he did not get my letter," Dianne interrupted, "but I did write one James. I left it with . . . what was her name . . . Pamela, yes, Pamela. I told her to give it to him as soon as he arrived," she explained, looking perplexed.

"I am sorry, but it did not reach him. Dianne, there is something you may not know." I clenched my teeth and took a deep breath. "There were a series of events that unfolded after you left. Pamela, it seems, was jealous of Michael as she had a crush on you."

Dianne took a sharp intake of breath. "Oh, good heavens. I know she flirted with me, but that was all."

"Well, it was enough not to give Michael your letter, and that may have been the only tragedy, but, I am afraid there is more, a lot more, you have not heard about. She was the one who told him you were pregnant." Dianne sat up looking perplexed.

"Michael told me he had had words with the Australian girl, Pamela, and another man who lived on the top floor. Do you remember him?" I asked, hoping she could.

Dianne continued to look thoughtful, and was obviously remembering, but what version of events would she reveal to me.

"Yes, I do . . . Martin . . . something, I think he was a law student. I didn't see much of him, although we did go to one of his party's while I was with Michael. I think he had a crush on me as well." She smiled, talking a little more freely now, staring nowhere in particular, but then turned to look at me. "But I do remember Pamela. She was a lesbian, and she did have her eye on me, but I was not interested. We got on otherwise, and I thought she was a friend. I trusted her with my letter to Michael. She must have kept it from him on purpose, out of spite, as you said."

A look of realization crossed her face. "If only Michael had read my note he would have at least known I left for a reason, and not just run away. Poor man. That must have been hard for him. The bitch. I could kill her for that." And thumped her fists into each other.

"Dianne, I am afraid someone has already done that," I said too eagerly, not knowing why I suggested murder instead of an accident.

"What! I knew nothing of that. When was this? What happened to her?" she asked, bewildered by my revelations.

"Well, she was found a month after you left. She had been smoking pot and drinking, and may have been taking anti-depressants."

"But you said murder. It sounds like an accident."

"Yes, sorry. The police report was inconclusive. The police officer in charge, however, kept the case open; suspecting either Michael or Martin had had a hand in her death."

Dianne sighed, and leant back in her chair with a look of concern and confusion, and I felt there was no point in saying any more just then until she had time to come to terms with what I had just revealed. She had spent the last forty years thinking she had done the right thing, but now the shock of knowing she had left Michael with the knowledge that she was running away because she was carrying his child was a lot to contemplate, and come to terms with.

I searched for a tissue and wiped my brow. "Your letter, Dianne, what was actually in it, if I may ask?" Wanting her to verify the contents Peter Wilkes had recalled to me.

She sighed, having gained some composure. "Oh, a lame excuse that I had to go home or something like that. Certainly not that I was pregnant. I did intend to return, I do know that James," she said sadly, recollecting her actions from all that time ago, and blinked away a tear.

After a couple of minutes, I asked. "The young girl . . . Lucie . . . who is she?"

Dianne said nothing at first, but she realized I knew too much already to turn me away. "She is my granddaughter. My Kimberly's child," she said quietly. "As you know more about me than most people, I will tell you my story but on one condition."

"Yes, of course," I said willingly.

"You do not repeat any of it to Michael Parker. As far as he is concerned I am dead, or you did not find me. Do you understand me, James," she said in such a forthright manner, I had to agree then and there.

"As you know I had Kimberly, and yes it was his child. I was young and just starting out on my wonderful career. A career I had planned for years. To travel the world and find beautiful and exotic objects. How could I do that with a child?" she paused to compose herself. "Some of that damn Catholic schooling must have crept under my skin. That is all I can think of," and she gave me half-smile.

"That's what Sinead said," but regretted the interruption.

"I eventually took Kimberly with me to Cairo, after Paris . . . did you find Louis by the way?"

"Yes, we did . . . he was a very nice gentleman and was very entertaining . . . and he still has an eye for the ladies." I added jovially.

Dianne smiled and nodded in agreement. "He was a charming man, and I was unkind to him as well. I thought he would have persuaded me to stay in Paris, probably ask me to marry him, and I was afraid I might, so I left a week early, just before Christmas, and later set-sail for Cairo."

She took a sip of now lukewarm tea, and I smiled at a thought. "I learnt of your liking for Earl Grey, and how you got your nickname, Lady Grey."

She laughed at the tale. "Yes, I was given the name by Rafi," she confirmed. "Tea has always been my weakness," she said, pouring a fresh cup. "So, let me continue, and then we will have lunch. During my stay in India I met my husband, Philippe. He was the *chargé d'affaires*, at the Spanish Embassy. We were invited to many Embassy receptions and balls in those days. They were a welcome break from the sun and dust of the digs."

Dianne was talking freely now and seemed to enjoy the good memories. Then she sighed at a not so good memory. "Kimberley adjusted well to life "on the road". She got a unique education I think and was a bright clever girl. She joined Reuters in 1985 as a photographer, and a few years later met and married fellow Reuters journalist, Stefan. They were a great team, both professionally and personally." She stood and fetched two framed photographs from the other room.

"This was taken on their wedding day in Prague, and this one a few weeks before they died, in Belgrade in 1999."

Both photos showed a smiling happy young couple and it was so sad to hear they had died.

"I am so sorry, Dianne. I did not know that. We tried to trace her but found nothing. What happened to them?"

Dianne sat back on the chair but leant forward this time, looking directly at me.

"They had been covering many of the conflicts of the time in the 1990's. There were many, which seemed never-ending. I was fearful like any mother would be, but they always came home. They covered the Gulf war and went to Sierra Leone, Algeria and of course the Bosnian and Kosovo Wars."

She fingered the photo frames lovingly. "They were due out of Belgrade as NATO had decided to intensify air-strikes. Reuters tried to get a message to them to evacuate, or at least find secure cover with other journalists. This they did, and were taken by a Chinese journalist to the Chinese Embassy in Belgrade for safety." She looked away from me, but I said nothing. I needed to hear all of this.

"On 7th May 1999 NATO bombed the Embassy killing three Chinese journalists, together with Kimberly and Stefan." She wiped away a tear. "Sorry, I have not talked about this for a long time. Not since Lucie was eight years old, and we decided to tell her about her parents."

Now I remember where I had seen the likeness to Lucie before, in the photo Sinead had shown me of Dianne. "She is pretty. Obviously runs in the family." I said in all innocence.

She looked back at me, head slightly cocked. "Do you have any Irish in you, James?"

"Not as far as know," I said blushing.

Dianne put back the silver-framed photos and brought over a book." This was hers. She had it published in 1995. Images of her life as a journalist. She won awards for her photography."

It was a heavy coffee-table book, case bound in a thick black cover, but with a beautiful embossed mosaic pattern covering both front and back of the book. Many of the images depicted the horrors of war. Why do black and white intensify the terror even more? Not all were of war zones. Beautiful landscapes, animals, buildings and even food. "It's lovely," is all I could say, which it was.

"So," she said sitting back in the chair, "that is my story. I have not been proud of some of the things I have done, but they are outweighed by the good things. My husband and I are still very much in love, and we are blessed with a beautiful granddaughter. I hope I have filled in any missing pieces for your research James." She picked up The Letter and handed it back to me. "You will need to return this to its owner, James."

I was going to have to decide how much to tell Michael Parker. I stayed for lunch, and Lucie joined us, who, I learnt, wanted to be a photographer.

Chapter Twenty One

On the flight home, I thought about what I would say to Michael Parker. Am I duty-bound to report the truth as he asked me to? What difference will it make to his state of health, or mind? Could he change his Will in favor of Dianne or even Lucie over his son, Charlie?

I had also promised Dianne I would say nothing of finding her. A dilemma I need to talk over with someone else - someone divorced from the circumstances surrounding my quest.

. . .

I only visit mother a few times a year now she and her new husband have moved to Solihull. They bought a good size detached property (they had to consider my grandparents) with a large garden, which keeps mum busy. I called to say I was coming, firstly because I wanted to visit when he was not around, and secondly, I would be in trouble for not giving her time to cook.

Apart from gardening, cooking was her most pleasurable pastime. Although happy with most western menus, she still likes to make traditional recipes and snacks, especially for visitors.

Before I reached the front door I could smell the familiar aroma of the home-made ladoos, and if I wasn't mistaken lamb biryani.

"James, lovely to see you. What a nice surprise," mother said greeting me with a kiss, "and why are you alone. Where is your lovely Jayne?"

"Sorry, Mother, she has to work as well. I promise to bring her soon." I said, handing her a box of her favorite Sohan Halwa and the gift wrapped sari I bought in India.

"Oh, thank you, James. You do remember your mother sometimes then."

"Always. It's just a shame you are a long way from London now. How is it here?"

"It's fine. We are all fine, well apart from your Grandpa, but he is comfortable. Now, come on in and sit down. Nani is in the living room. I will fetch some food"

The large lounge was bright and tastefully decorated with a good mix of European and Asian influences, which I suspect would be attributed to my step-father. Our old house had very little in the way of Indian decor or art.

Nani was sitting on one of the large sofas wearing her best sari. "Hello nani, how are you?" I said, leaning over, kissing her gently.

"I am well as can be. Dadu is not so good, so go up and see him before you leave.

"Of course I will. I heard he was not feeling well. What is wrong with him?" I inquired with concern.

"Old age I think. We both suffer from the same problem," she said with a wrinkled smile.

Mother came in carrying a tray of snacks. "Just something before lunch," she said setting down enough food for several people.

"Mother, do you never learn. It's such a waste, all this just for us."

"You need it I think. Look at you. Is what you have been doing, flying off everywhere, making you lose weight?" Mother said, handing me a large plate of food, and nani nodding in agreement.

"So, how are my relatives? It was good of you to make time to visit them," mother said. "I have not seen Joji since we went over for his wedding."

"They are all fine, and it was good to meet them. I . . . I feel connected now . . . to my . . ." I didn't want to say roots, but it comes down to that in the end, ". . . relatives. I have photos to show you on the iPad later."

Mother frowned, and nani nodded. I felt deeply uncomfortable knowing what I did with nani sitting right in front of me. We ate in silence and I managed a couple of home-made kozhukkattas.

"So what was the urgent visit for on a Thursday without your lady?" Mother asked gleefully, looking at nani in a most disturbing way.

I put my plate down where mother could not fill it up. "Well, I wanted your advice on a delicate matter . . ."

"Oh yes, of course, my dear boy." Nani interrupted, with a renewed spirit I had not seen for some time. "Yes," she continued, looking at mother, "you are right to have concerns, but you can be assured we all have your best interests at heart. It's not like in your mother's time. Mixed marriages then were frowned upon, and even your dadu was not 100% in agreement, but we had started a new life in England and there were new ways to . . . why are you shaking your head like that my boy."

I could not believe it. They thought I had come for reassurance or their blessing to marry Jayne. I should have been cross, but mother suddenly looked very embarrassed, so I tried to soften the situation.

"Nani, mother . . . your concerns are very welcome with regards to Jayne and myself, but that is not why I have come to see you." I said, looking at mother directly.

Nani looked confused and stood up. "I will go and stir the biryani," and she left us alone.

"I am so sorry, James. We couldn't think why you wanted to come mid-week, and making sure Kamala is not at home. When, if . . . it does come to you and Jayne marrying, Kamala will be . . ." she struggled to say what she wanted . . . "he's very traditional James, but a good man. I wish you would get to know him better."

"Perhaps I will, if it makes you happy mother," and I moved over to sit next to her, and kissed her hand.

"Now, what is this other delicate matter," she said smiling.

I related most of the Michael Parker story, keeping it as short as possible, and sat back for her reaction. She took my hand. "You are a good boy James. Kind, considerate, thoughtful . . . and a little predictable," she said raising an eyebrow.

"What does that mean?" I said, looking hurt.

"Darling, I love it that you came and asked my advice, but we both know you have already made-up your own mind as to what you will tell Mr Parker."

I sighed and leant back on the sofa. "Have you always seen through me?" I said, feeling deflated.

"James, don't think that. You always do the right thing. That is one of your qualities. Your gift."

She was right of course. I was not going to tell Michael Parker anything. I will report to him all the people I have met and places visited in this marathon search, but in the end, Dianne Holland was elusive.

I arrived at Michael Parker's house and knew instinctively something was wrong. There were at least six cars parked in the drive and more in the road. The front door was opened by Mrs Smith who smiled politely and ushered me in. "How is he?" I asked.

"As comfortable as he can be. Charlie and the doctor are with him just now, but he has been asking for you."

I nodded in reply, not knowing what to say. I saw then on the hall table a letter addressed to Morris, Sterne and Wicks, handwritten in the same neat copperplate script that had written the name Dianne on the envelope of The Letter.

"That's a neat hand Mr Parker has," I said, still eyeing the envelope.

"Oh, no, I . . ." then she stopped, realizing what I was getting at. She smiled coyly, and I turned to see she must have been crying earlier. "I'm sorry, it's just that I have known Mr Parker for over thirty years, and . . . well . . . one can't help . . ." and she closed her eyes and looked down.

"It's to be expected," I said. "It's a sad time," hoping to ease her anxiety. But I did want to know something. "Did you write the letter?" I asked as casually as possible.

Mrs Smith looked back at me and smiled gently, nodding. "Yes, I did. He dictated it and asked me to write it. He would never have managed it, poor man."

"So, you knew the story before anyone else? What did you think?"

She turned away to check if anyone had come out of the sitting room. "I was shocked at first, but Michael said he needed to know the truth. He swore me to secrecy, not to tell anyone, especially Charlie. He could see I was upset but how could I refuse him after all these years. They have been a wonderful couple to work for and they have treated me like one of the family." She said wiping another tear away.

"So," she said, regaining her composure. "What did you find out about Dianne Holland?"

I opened my briefcase and took out The Letter. Her eyes opened wide and she gave a gasp of relief, holding her chest, and I thought she was going to collapse on me. "I hope this answers your question, Mrs Smith. Please take it. I believe you may want to . . . bury the past once again."

Her hand was trembling slightly, but she took the now shabby envelope from me. "Thank you, Mr Lacey. That is very thoughtful," she said quietly, her voice still quivering, and leant over and kissed my cheek.

Just then a gentleman I had not seen before came into the hall. "Are you James, he asked.

"Yes, I am."

"I am Mr Parker's doctor. He is very weak but said he needs to see you. Please do not be long or excite him."

I entered the same dimly lit room I had been interviewed in on my first visit just as Charlie Parker was leaving. I nodded, but said nothing, seeing his expression was one of annoyance. The room was laid out differently. Michael's bed had been set up here, and there was a mountain of medical paraphernalia on the table, with a drip and oxygen lines entering him from all angles.

He opened his eyes and smiled.

"Sorry you have to see me like this, James, but I wanted to thank you for what you have done for me. It has meant a lot."

"Mr Parker, sir, I am sorry about your condition now, it must be difficult."

"Nonsense, my boy," he said trying to sit up more. I lifted the pillow until he looked more comfortable. "I expected it, and planned this. No sterile hospital room for me. Family and friends are all I need." He paused, wanting to ask the most important question. "So, tell me, James, did you fulfil an old man's dream?"

. . .

Mrs Smith was alone in the kitchen. Although it was large and had been modernized from time to time, it still had a small wood burner centerpiece, which was working well on this cold November day.

She fingered her own neat writing and gently folded the envelope in two. She opened the front grill of the fire and placed, almost reverently, the envelope into the flames for cremation, giving her closure on the subject of Dianne Holland.

. . .

I closed the lounge the door quietly, leaving Michael with the knowledge I had been unsuccessful in finding his memories. He had learned back on the pillow and closed his eyes, and I took my leave. Three days later Mrs

Smith called my office to say Michael had passed away and would I like to attend the burial at Bunhill Graveyard the following Tuesday morning.

. . .

Charlie Parker was not happy to learn his father had requested a verse on his headstone. Especially as he had learned it was dedicated to someone he had never met and took it as an insult to his late mother's memory.

Before Michael died he tried to explain to Charlie what he had asked James Lacey to do, but Charlie was horrified to learn his dying wish was to find a lover from over forty years past.

"Go see a Priest if you want absolution, Dad!" He had shouted at his father. "How can you even think about someone else after all these years? Did you never love mother? What about me. Did you did love me, and you're Grandchildren? What do I tell them?"

Michael had known it was going to be difficult explaining what James had been doing all those months, but had predicted his son's reaction. Perhaps he should have said nothing. He was weak now, and knew he only had a short time left, but did not want them to part with any ill feeling or misunderstanding between them.

"Sit down, Charlie I want to talk to you. I cannot do that while you are pacing the room."

Charlie eventually sat next to the bed. His expression somber.

"Charlie, I want you to know, as I am sure you do already, I do love you and always have done. I have, and always will, love your mother." Charlie went to speak but Michael raised his limp hand. "Wait, son, let me finish and then you can have your say if you still feel the same." Charlie relented but still looked at this father gravely.

"What I asked Mr Lacey to do was follow an instinct I had, an almost nagging feeling that I needed to find someone I knew a long time ago. I had no idea if they were alive or where they lived." He paused for breath, but also to see if his son was going to interrupt again. He did not, so Michael continued. "When I was diagnosed with this cancer, I knew I had not long to live. I have had a good life, a beautiful and loving wife, and a son I am proud of, and two wonderful grandchildren." He paused again but this time because his eyes were swelling as he started to reminisce.

"As we get older, and find we are dying, memories are precious to us. You relive your life in episodes, starting as far back as you can. Childhood, school days, teenager years, first job, and of course, lovers and relationships."

Charlie shifted in his seat, feeling uneasy at what was to come "Dad, I really don't want to know about your love life all that time ago."

Michael interrupted. "Son, I won't embarrass you, I promise." Charlie could see the emotion in his father's eyes and relaxed back in his chair.

"Memories can play tricks. Something you think you had forgotten, or what was hiding at the back of your mind for many years suddenly starts to edge nearer to the front," he paused, choosing his words carefully. "When I was diagnosed, these memories started to reappear. Had your mother been alive, I promise you, son, I would not have pursued them. As it is, I have left the business to you and shared out my estate to deserving causes and some close friends, and of course, my grandchildren. However, I wanted to know for certain if this person was alive, and if they were, if they were in need of financial help."

Charlie stepped in. "I assume this lady has a name." His tone was more relaxed and part of him was now intrigued as to why his father wanted to confess after all these years.

Michael sighed. "Her name is not important to you. Especially now I have been told she cannot be found. Mr Lacey has done exhaustive research and travelled, on my behalf, to several countries to establish her whereabouts. Now I have told him to discontinue his search after his visit today. You see son, I have exorcised my demon and I am free." He leant back on his pillow and closed his eyes.

Charlie was still confused and many questions were running through his mind. "But, Dad, I don't understand why you wanted to find her after so long. Did you want to see her again? Did you have unfinished business? Did you leave her? Was she pregnant?" With each question Charlie was edging closer to Michael until he was just a few inches from his face. Looking him straight in the eyes and firing questions. The last question caused a reaction. Michael looked away.

"So, she was pregnant ... and you left her."

"No!" Michael turned suddenly and Charlie shot back in the chair. "No, I did not leave her. She left me, son. She left without saying anything or leaving a note. That's the big mystery I have been trying to unfold." He closed his eyes and controlled his breathing. "Why did she leave me?" He whispered over and over; drained of memories, and the overwhelming desire to sleep.

Chapter Twenty Two

I wrote to Dianne soon afterwards and told her Michael had passed away, not really expecting to hear from her again, and I was, therefore, surprised to receive a letter back a week later.

She said she was to be in London in a couple of weeks and would like to meet up, and would I visit the grave with her.

"Do you think she is feeling guilty now?" Jayne asked.

I stretched my arms and rubbed my eyes. I was feeling mentally, and physically tired. I had travelled halfway around the world and found not only answers for Michael Parker, but I had also discovered things that affected me, and my life. Questions that I need to address sometime.

"Sorry love, I was miles away," I replied putting down Dianne's letter and joining Jayne on the sofa. "I don't think so. Maybe in the very beginning, but now, all these years later she may have regrets, but I think that is different to guilt."

Jayne looked sideways at me. "What!" I asked.

"I love you, James Lacey." And she kissed me ever so tenderly.

"Tell me what I did and I will do it again," I whispered.

"Just be you . . . not someone you are expected to be," she said, leaning back in the corner of the sofa.

"Is this to do with what I told you about India?" I asked, but I knew the answer.

"Yes it was interesting to see my relatives, and yes it did make me think about what Joji said about heritage and taking paths, but I am not making any life-changing decisions . . . and not without talking to you about it when the time is right."

Jayne hugged me and held me close for some time, and when she released me, I could see a tear line running down her cheek.

"What's all that for?" I asked reassuringly.

"I don't want to lose you, James," she said desperately. "I love you the way you are. I am sorry if that sounds mean or unfair, or . . . ," she raised her hands in frustration searching for a word . . . "egotistic, but that's how I feel." And she rested her head on my chest and cried.

"Hey, Jayne, look at me. I love you too. I am not going anywhere soon, and I am not going to turn into a Buddhist Monk . . . anyway, orange isn't my color."

She stifled a laugh, and wiped her eyes. "I didn't say anything about a Buddhist Monk, but you know what I mean, and that's good."

We sat there a while longer just holding each other, and I knew then of one path I wanted to take.

. . .

Two weeks later as planned, Dianne and her granddaughter, Lucie, came to London, and we agreed to meet them at the Cemetery on the following day at 1.00pm, 27th November. I had emailed the directions as this was no ordinary cemetery. Bunhill Graveyard is, in fact, a little-known oasis in the heart of London. Its history goes back as far as Saxon times, and in 1685 was used to bury the dead from the Plague when other cemeteries were full. It was in use until 1855, and has some notable residents including William Blake, Daniel Defoe and John Bunyan. Now, for the first time in over 100 years, Michael Parker has bought a six by four plot, when no one else had been granted permission - how he achieved this no one knows, except Mr Morris and the City of London Council, the current owners of the land.

That Friday morning when we woke, we knew something was different. It was quiet outside. No cars, no school children shouting. It could only mean one thing. We scrambled to the window and pulled back the curtain like a couple of kids on Christmas Day. The brightness of the sky and the whiteness of the snow nearly blinded us.

"Bugger," I said out loud, "that's going to slow things down."

"Great, can we go back to bed and cuddle up for the rest of day. No point in getting stranded out there." Jayne said with some degree of seriousness.

Under normal circumstances, I would have agreed. Nothing better than snuggling up on a cold winters day, but we had an arrangement which could, and should not be broken.

"Sorry love, but I have to meet her, and I would like you to be there as well, seeing you have been on most of this journey with me."

Jayne looked at me from behind the warm quilt, with those come to bed eyes. "OK, James, if it means that much to you, of course, I will, and I suppose

I do have a sneaking curiosity as to what she is like; this mystery woman who has taken you from me for several months.”

I sat beside her on the bed. “You will like her. She is … very … elegant.” Is all I could think of, although that in itself is not a fair and true reflection. Our Dianne Greenway is indeed a mix of many things; mysterious, clever, calculating, romantic, rich … and elegant.

How different would her life have been if she had stayed with Michael Parker? Would she have pursued her chosen career and travelled the world … yes, I think she may have.

She had a determination and spirit, maybe born out of wanting to leave Ireland, but, nonetheless, a determination that would have taken her far.

 “Hey, dreamer,” Jayne said, poking me in the ribs.

“Sorry, just thinking about what the past few months have meant to me and some of the people I have met. It's about making decisions, isn't it?

Hoping that the decisions we make, either on the spur of the moment or calculated, will be the right ones. Dianne made a life-changing decision but she won through in the end. Yes, it is sad she has lost a daughter, but that was nothing to do with her original decision in leaving, and I feel fortunate to have been on this journey of discovery for Michael, as well as myself.”

I leant over a kissed Jayne on the lips. “If after all this time, we had found she had died I think I would have felt cheated, not knowing how her life was, or what her reasons were for leaving.”

“Hey,” Jayne lifted my sunken head. “She is alive, and I think you have done a wonderful job. I know how you like to analyze everything James, and that is admirable, but it can make you very morose and …”

“And what!” I wanted to know.

“. . . boring,” she said laughing out loud and grabbing my sides and tickling me, which she knows is not something I like.

I rolled onto her and we kissed.

“Sorry,” I said. “I did not mean to be a bore; I suppose I just was thinking about how I hope the choices I make will be the right ones.”

We kissed again and found we had a least another half-an-hour before getting dressed.

. . .

By the time we reached the graveyard entrance it had stopped snowing, and we waited for Dianne to arrive, trying to keep warm. Jayne held my arm and pulled me close. "I promise you a warming meal after this wherever you want to go." I said, hoping to take her mind off the weather. "Maybe we could go up the Shard," I suggested, remembering many people have proposed on the 69th floor, overlooking the City of London.

Before she could answer, however, a chauffeur-driven black 750i BMW pulled up beside us, and the driver came around to open the rear passenger door next to where we were standing. He offered his hand, and Dianne took it to steady herself as she got out of the car.

She looked stunning. Long fur coat with matching hat and leather gloves. She greeted me like a long-lost friend. "James, so nice to see you again." And she kissed me on each cheek.

"Dianne, sorry about bringing you out in this," I said, just for something to say. She turned to Jayne. "This must be the lovely Jayne I have heard so much about."

Jayne looked surprised and shot me a look that said I was in trouble. "Yes, lovely to meet you as well, and likewise, I have heard a lot about you," Jayne replied, shaking Dianne's hand.

"Well, we girls must compare notes sometime, Jayne. You know what it is like when men try to "relate" stories," she said, putting Jayne at ease, but making me a little nervous.

"So," I interrupted, wanting to get this over with, "shall we go in?"

"Yes, of course, James. It's getting colder now. Jayne, you look cold my dear. Why don't you sit in the car with my granddaughter, Lucie, and keep warm?

"Thank you that would be good," Jayne said eagerly, and before she could move the chauffeur had opened the door for her.

"Keep the engine running for them will you?" Jayne said to the driver.

"So, James," Jayne said," take my arm and lead the way." I obeyed, and felt the warmth of the soft fur tingle my fingers, and felt instantly warmer.

We walked the few yards along the center path dividing the graveyard in two, until we came to an iron gate, gaining entrance to the private grounds and burial plots the public would not normally be allowed to see close up.

Michael Parker, for all his money, only managed to secure a small corner plot, but made up for it by funding a seven-foot marble obelisk.

As we approach the site, Dianne stopped and put a hand to her mouth. "What is it?" I said, "Are you OK, do you want to go on?"

"Yes, yes my dear boy. I was just surprised, or perhaps should not have been, to see the obelisk. The dear man. He still remembered how we met all those years ago, and he actually had one made as a headstone - the obelisk of Hatshepsut. It's amazing."

We walked slowly, although the snow had much to do with that, closer and closer to the foot of the grave. Snow had covered much of the graveyard, and only those plots with headstones or the larger tombs could be seen above snow level.

I stepped back to give Dianne some privacy, but she did not want me to move. "No, please stay, James. I think you have earned the right to be here, maybe above anyone else outside of the family." She spoke quietly, and with respect, looking all the time at the obelisk. "I cannot make out the inscription James. Would you be a dear and clear the snow off for me."

I walked forward wishing I had brought my gloves, but surprisingly the soft new snow fell away easily from the front of the stone needle revealing the mason's work.

"Damn." Dianne pulled a small white handkerchief from her pocket. "I promised myself I would not do that." And wiped a tear from the corner of her left eye. "He really loved that man, didn't he?" she said reading the inscription and text by Leonard Cohen.

In loving memory of a Husband, Father and Granddad

Michael Richard Parker

Born 1947

Ring the bells that still can ring
Forget your perfect offering
There is a crack in everything
That's how the light gets in

"It's not unusual at places like this," I said, trying to sound reassuring.

"Bless you, James, but it was seeing that verse again. We both loved Cohen. He was a poet and Michael was a pure romantic. He brought me four LPs of his in the six months we were together, and I still have them . . . somewhere."

I let her remember the good things about their brief relationship.

"Do you think you did the right thing by not letting me tell him about your daughter?"

She turned and smiled. "Absolutely, James, absolutely. It was the right decision, and one I took a very long time ago.

I may have been wrong then, I don't know, but at the time I only knew I could not face him again having had Kimberly. Not after the wonderful time we had. If I was to break his heart this was the least painful way."

I smiled, not sure what to say. I knew the full story and did not stand in judgment. That was not for me to do. I have played my part and been grateful for the experience gained, and for the places I have visited, and for the people I have met.

We turned and walked slowly back to the car. "Are you going to marry that lovely lady of yours, James?"

"You know, I think I was about to propose just as you arrived."

Dianne smiled and hid any sign of surprise she may have had.

As we approached the car the driver opened the rear door to let Jayne out. As she stepped out of the car she leant down and said, "Goodbye – it's been fun meeting you."

Dianne held out her hand to me and leant forward and kissed me on the cheek. "Thank you for being here, James. It was good of you."

Dianne turned and stepped a pace closer to Jayne, and gave her a gentle kiss on the left cheek. "Take care of him, my dear. I hope you will be very happy together."

She then leant into the back seat and lifted out a large Jute carrier bag with rope handles.

"Here, James, this is for you. A little memento."

"That's not necessary, Dianne. Michael gave me . . ."

Dianne put a finger to my lips. "Quiet. Know how to accept graciously, James."

I parted the layers of colored tissue covering the heavy object, but my heart was already pounding. "It's a . . ."

"Gift," Dianne interjected and whispered in my ear. "It's my wedding gift." And she was in the car before I could argue further.

The powerful BMW engine purred silently through the snow, and turned the corner.

Jayne and I looked at each other. "Did that go OK, what did she say?" Jayne asked, eager to know.

I smiled and shrugged. "I think she has laid her past to rest."

Jayne looked at the object we had been given. "It's a vase," Jayne said, "how lovely," and gently lifted the pure white round Moon Jar out of the bag. Her gaze turned to a frown when she saw the crack.

"Hey, James, it's cracked."

I just smiled and said, "That's how the light gets in."

We walked on to find warmth and sustenance, with Jayne still trying to work out what I had meant.

"James, what did Dianne whisper to you?"

"Sorry, client confidentiality my love."

"James, I can tickle you every night, all night if you want me to . . ."

"She said it was a wedding present."

"That's nice . . . who is getting married?"

THE END

Acknowledgements

Thank you again to all my friends and family for their encouragement and help writing this second novel.

Special thanks again to dear friend Ros McCaul for the re-reads and valued comments, and editing my obvious errors.

To John Mackenzie for his legal input. Our friend Sinead who was a great help with the Irish names.

To the wonderful Bastian family, George and Gina, who I stayed with at their Homestay in Fort Cochin, Kerala. (A great place to chill-out).

Reference to The Nude Murders relates to a police investigation between 1959 and 1965 when a total of eight women were found murdered in the borough and in neighboring Chiswick and Brentford. The murderer was never caught and the case files remain closed.

The Seven Songs of Merlin by T. A. Barron reproduced with kind permission from Penguin Books.

The Princess Ora where Dianne was rescued from was based on the Empress of Britain who was lost off the coast of Ireland when attacked on October 26, 1940 first by a German aircraft and two days later by a U-boat which itself was sunk two days afterwards by a British destroyer. It was the largest liner lost in the war and although there was not a heavy loss of life, as was often the case during the war news of its loss was censored since it was such a significant ship.

Addition information on the author can be found at:
www.davidbalaam-books.co.uk

Other titles by the same author;

Columbus Day

Nothing is Sacrosanct

No One is Sacrosanct

Read the beginning of this new and complex thriller . . . dark, romantic, brutal . . . contains adult subjects.

190

NOTHING IS SACROSANCT

by

David E Balaam

To all the innocent victims . . .

may your voices be heard one day

PART ONE

Chapter One

1969

Daniel Mace stirred from his induced sleep. His vision was blurred, his head was throbbing with pain and he could feel a burning sensation on the side of his neck. Somewhere in the distance, he thought he could hear the faint sound of laughter and clapping. His eyes, still blurred, picked out the lined red, green and brown flocked pattern wallpaper on the stairs, although, something within his numb cerebral cortex, combined with his blurred vision, couldn't remember the pattern having a brown stripe. He blinked several times to focus, and it took a few moments for the adrenaline to kick in - and it did, as soon as he realized his predicament. Daniel Mace was tied and gagged, sitting on the first-floor landing of his house looking directly at a brown rope hanging from the open loft door – unmistakably a hangman's noose.

He looked around in fear, trying to call out to no avail. The first glimpse of his abductor was when the bathroom door opened. "Hello, Daniel. Sorry to keep you waiting." Said a cold calculated voice.

Daniel Mace murmured uncontrollably, not knowing what on-earth this intruder was talking about. The stranger, with an unusual accent and polite smile, stood in front of Mace for a few moments looking at the pathetic man; pleased with himself he had achieved this much. He was now sure the final act would go smoothly, and his undertaking would be complete. The stranger sat opposite Mace and leaned back against the wooden landing uprights. He crossed his legs, looking relaxed as he re-stretched the Latex gloves on each hand whilst giving Mace a disturbing smile. "Daniel," he finally said, in a measured tone, "let me tell you why I am here." The stranger's face tightened and his smile dissolved. "You've been naughty, haven't you, Daniel. Very naughty."

Chapter Two

1979 December

Marcus was lying on his bed, naked, allowing Rosa to give him a massage. "I was thinking of Isabel and Charlie," he said casually. Rosa stopped massaging his unique hairless chest. She was also naked, straddling his lower abdomen, his penis partially erect due to the massaging. Rosa looked at Marcus suspiciously. "You said it was a one-off, no more. You promised," she said, with a concerned that touched Marcus. He leaned forward and cupped her face with his right hand. "I thought you liked them. You said they were willing and responsive . . . your words, my angel." Rosa sighed and took hold of Marcus's semi-erect penis and started to massage it. She worked her hand up and down expertly, as she had been taught, and he remembered how he had found her, and how much fun it had been teaching her many things, just those five short years ago.

His thoughts drifted back to his youth and his family, and those black times during the war. He placed his hand over Rosa's hand. "Not there. Not just now, my love," he said, somberly. Rosa nodded, and returned to work on his chest, pouring warm scented oil on his stomach, then working her hands rhythmically over his glistening torso. He let Rosa continue her expert manipulation as he closed his eyes, remembering, as he did from time to time, how lucky he had been, escaping from occupied Austria.

The allies'; Russia, France, America and Britain had divided his country into four zones. Marcus's family had lived in the south-east province of Styria, in the small village of Mariahof, which was in the British sector. Although remote, the allies quickly spread over the newly liberated state, and found the young Marcus alone in his parent's large country Schloss. The commanding officer who came upon the isolated house that day in June 1945 found a woman hanging from the kitchen rafters. Further inspection of the rooms found a young boy aged about ten years old, shivering and hiding in one of the bedrooms' dressing rooms, huddled behind a row of women's dresses. The officer who found him asked him his name. The boy had said nothing, preferring to stare into space, squatting on the floor with arms folded, shivering and afraid.

The boy was taken to an internment camp where he was cleaned and fed and then interrogated by British military officers, in particular a Major Ferris. However, at all the interviews, even with German speaking personnel, the boy refused to answer any questions. A few weeks later

Marcus was informed his father had been captured by the Russians and executed as an SS Officer. Marcus showed no emotion on receiving this news, but inwardly was joyous and relieved that he was now also free of his father, but wondered why there was no word from his brother. Surely, now the war was over, Marius would come and take him home where they would be safe, and play together like they did when he was younger.

They questioned Marcus for days, wanting to know how his mother hanged herself, especially as her hands had been cut off at the wrists. Marcus acted the dumb orphan and just stared at his accusers with his bright steel blue eyes until they realized the interrogation was going nowhere.

As a minor, his captors were undecided what to do with him. Several translators were unable to get anything out of him, and stopped short of beating him. Later, Marcus thanked God he had not been in the Russian or American sectors – he was not sure how he would have fared with their interrogation methods.

After four weeks of intensive questioning, an army doctor intervened. He had been supervising Marcus's condition since his arrival, and insisted on being present during the questioning. He also spoke some German so was able to communicate with Marcus on a different level, as a friend, rather than an inquisitor. He would bring chocolate bars and treats to Marcus in his dormitory and talk to him quietly, gaining his trust. Marcus distrusted any close associations after his enslavement by his parents. He assumed all adults were child molesters, no matter how caring they seemed to be.

But Dr.Nathan Star was kind and compassionate to Marcus, and slowly gained his trust. He gave him errands to run and tried to keep him busy, until he gradually succumbed to a more normal way of life, if that was even possible in what was nothing less than a detention camp for displaced people.

After a while, Dr Star gave him a job as an orderly in the medical unit. There he had access to fresh clothes, regular hot meals and even started to interact with other normal decent people. By now he had learnt some English and was able to converse a little - with those he chose to. The population of the displacement camp dwindled over-time when relatives had been found or they were allowed to leave having been cleared of any atrocities. One day Dr Star took Marcus to one side. "Marcus, they want to hand you over to the police, in Vienna." Dr Star spoke slowly so Marcus could understand what he was being told. "The death of your mother is still unexplained, but Major Ferris says it is now a civil matter."

"I will not go," is all Marcus would say, looking Dr Star defiantly in the eyes.

Rosa was still massaging him, and he sighed with pleasure at her gentle touch.

Dr Nathan Star had argued on behalf of Marcus as to why the boy was to be handed over, but he was stone-walled every time. "Don't interfere, doctor. See to the sick." Was the retort from the commanding officer.

Dr Star's tour of duty was coming to an end and he was looking forward to going home – back to his wife and five year old daughter, Barbara, whom he had not seen for over a year.

The day came. Several of his colleagues were travelling with him and they were to depart by bus to Graz, then a plane to Berne, and finally a flight back to London. Accompanying them were two gravely wounded men; one a soldier and one a civilian, who needed urgent treatment at the Queen Victoria Hospital, East Grinstead in England, where new and successful techniques were being carried out on burns victims. However, the day before departure the young civilian patient died in the middle of the night from trauma. Dr Star was called but nothing could be done for the young man, but there was something he could do for someone else.

With the help of a trusted nurse they swapped the identities of the dead patient with Marcus's, and bandaged Marcus's face and arms so he could not be recognized. Six medical staff and two patients left the camp the following day as planned, and arrived back in England four days later. As Marcus's stretcher was carried out to the waiting truck, an orderly was overheard to say, "Blimey, this guy weighs a ton."

Marcus stayed with Dr Star and his family in Surrey as their adopted son, although nothing was officially recorded. He went to the local school and sung in the church choir, and was very quick to learn. By the time he was eighteen he was fluent in five languages and had a good head for maths. In 1953 an old friend of Dr Star, who worked at the London Stock Exchange, took Marcus on as an apprentice 'Trader'.

A few days after Dr Star's departure, Major Ferris requested his sergeant to bring Marcus to him for transfer to Vienna, but was informed he could not be found.

"What do you mean, sergeant? He has to be here somewhere. Bring me Doctor Star." He bellowed. The Sergeant seemed unmoved by his superiors' outburst. "Sir, Dr Star left four days ago to return to the UK. His replacement has not arrived yet."

Ferris stared momentarily, analyzing this information. "Who left with him, sergeant?"

"Doctor Freeman, nurse Anne Cowell, Nurse Sally Peters, anesthetist Raymond Smith and two patients on stretchers, being transferred to a burns hospital in England, sir."

"What were their names?" Ferris asked.

"Private Banner and an Austrian civilian, Herr Rosenberg. He was badly burnt in a fire two weeks ago if you remember, sir." Ferris sat thoughtfully tapping his fingers on the desk. "Sergeant, do a thorough search for Marcus von Hartstein. He has to be somewhere in this camp."

Nathan Star and his wife were the only ones who knew Marcus's true story, and they took it with them to their graves when they died in a car crash in 1956. Marcus knew he would tell Rosa, as he had Barbara, the same story one day – when the time was right.

It seemed longer than five years ago since Marcus had rescued Rosa from her own nightmare in Armenia, and wondered what would have happened to her if he had left her there to fend for herself.

He felt the warmth of Rosa as she maneuvered herself into him. "You were asleep I think," she said playfully. "What were you dreaming about? You started to mumble something."

"I was . . . remembering. I was remembering how lucky I have been. I do want to help those two young people, Isabel and Charlie, and I want you to help me. Will you do that for me, my dear Rosa?"

Rosa cocked her head to one side and smiled. "You know I cannot refuse you anything, Marcus. When do we start?"

Chapter Three

When the sun sets over the River Thames it is one of the most beautiful sights I have had the pleasure to witness, especially in the 'Golden Hour', as the sun dips low, bouncing off the glistening water at low tide; something I have photographed many times. The ice in my Martini has melted, but it still tastes good as I drain the residue and nibble on the sliver of lemon. I always remember him when I drink a Martini Vermouth; Marcus Hartmann, friend, lover, benefactor and . . . and . . . someone I really didn't know that well. Whatever life he lived, I only know him as a kind and gentle man. If he had secrets, which I am sure he did, then they have disappeared with him, wherever he is. From where I am sitting on the small patio of our Victorian terrace house in Barnes, contemplating reaching fifty in a few months, I can see the two large paintings he left Charlie and me, and, although I can't quite see it, I know the Chair is to my left, against the wall. The Chair that captivated me and seduced me. The Chair that taught me Free Will . . . The Chair that brought me into the world of Marcus Hartmann, back in 1979.

Now, continue the journey . . but be prepared to be shocked